Richard Carpenter's

ROBIN OF SHERWOOD

HERE BE DRAGONS

by Gary Russell

This first edition of
Here Be Dragons
published in 2021 by
Chinbeard Books
in association with
Spiteful Puppet Ltd
www.spitefulpuppet.com

Layout & adaptation for this print edition by
Andrews UK Limited
www.andrewsuk.com

CONTENTS

CHAPTER ONE

It was raining. Not the cold, wet downpour that soaked you in seconds and made you ache for hot mead and some warm straw to rest on, but that peculiarly English rain that's more like a mist that just hangs in the air. Instead of big splashes of water on your head, it's like a million little pinpricks of dampness that gets you soaked without realising it.

And makes the grass and leaves smell of winter.

Which would be fine if it wasn't late June. By now the sun should be up and about and the damp dankness of spring should be fading and giving way to summer.

Benjamin Hockleaf was already fed up with it. A grizzled veteran of army life, much of his 31 years had been spent in service to whoever was the master of the castle at Nottingham, which at the moment was Rainault, the Sheriff of Nottingham, placed into power at the behest of King John. Benjamin had learned a long time ago not to be anything other than a follower of the Sheriff. Those that showed the slightest degree of mistrust or question an order or decree tended to disappear into the night, never to be heard of again.

Benjamin Hockleaf was pretty determined to stay where he was and thus, he, for the most part, lived his life safely and obeyed orders.

But of course, every so often some hiccup occurred, and such a hiccup was why he was in Sherwood Forest today. In the rain. With a novice as his companion.

Sam was young, little more than a child really. He said he was 22 but he had the bearing – and facial spots – of someone much younger; Benjamin had little doubt Sam had lied about how many summers he'd so far seen to become part of the guard at the castle. Sam had travelled over from the Marches after most of the men in his area had been seconded to the Crusades some years ago. When he first arrived, he spoke a strange language that few in Nottingham could understand but Sam quickly learned to speak the same as Benjamin and the others, so that made him fit in a bit better.

Benjamin's reverie was broken when a splash occurred behind him, followed by a loud curse. He spun round, glaring at Sam.

'Quiet!' Benjamin snarled. 'Why can't you be quieter?'

'You try being quiet in this footwear,' Sam said indignantly, pointing at a leaky leather boot.

Benjamin sighed and shook his head. 'I am being quiet. In exactly the same footwear.'

'S'only a puddle,' muttered Sam. 'Sorry.'

Benjamin stopped walking and rested himself against a large tree, which singularly failed to shield him from the misty rain, which didn't help his mood further.

'Look Sam Tully, I don't want to be here any more than you do, but we have orders. Well, I do. You're just meant to be watching. And learning.'

Sam laughed quietly. 'Ohhh. "Learning how to get kicked out of the horse guards, isn't it" you mean?'

Benjamin glared at him. That was a low blow.

'I mean, you'd be back on 'orse duty now, tomorrow, if you hadn't been so clumsy, wouldn't you?'

'It wasn't my fault Gisburne knocked into me.'

Sam laughed. 'Oh no, never your fault. Same as it weren't you fault the mead then splashed onto the Sheriff's boots. An' oooh bach, the look on Sir Guy's face when he thought he might get the blame.'

Benjamin shrugged. 'Gave me a look of pure poison. It was like staring into the face of a snake.'

Sam nodded. 'They don't call him Sir Hiss for nothing, do they now? I mean, he is a snake, nasty snake.'

Benjamin thought it was time to instil a bit of discipline into proceedings. 'Now, don't you be saying that about Sir Guy out loud, Sam Tully. He's your lord and master, you wanted to work for him and the other nobles at court. You have a bit of respect, right?'

Sam nodded, chastised. 'Sorry Benjamin.'

Benjamin pushed himself away from the tree and pointed further into the thick green – and decidedly damp – foliage of the forest. 'Now come on, we're supposed to be finding Robin Hood's camp.' He walked off, allowing himself a slight smile, unseen by Sam Tully, at the nickname of "Sir Hiss" for Guy of Gisburne. Because it was very apt.

***

Robin wondered why he'd never started counting the days it rained in Sherwood Forest.

Then he wondered why he was wondering that in the first place. It wasn't as though it was something he could change. He and his friends had done a lot of things over the years that involved causing change. The weather wasn't one of them. And whilst the likes of Will and even Much would sit and moan about the weather, especially in late Spring, Robin saw no point in complaining about things that couldn't be changed and affected or altered in any way. You might just as well ask why the moon comes out as night or why dogs chase rats. The answer is always "because they do". Same with rain.

Robin lay back onto the ground and stared upwards, blinking away the misty rain as it touched his face, staring up at the light grey sky above. He put his tongue out – he could taste the rain and through it, he could taste the forest around him. Each shade of green and brown, each flower and leaf, each blade of grass and fern, they all tasted different and they were all contained within the rain.

Nature. And he and his band were at the heart of it all. They had been living in Sherwood Forest for, Robin wasn't sure how long, but a few years now. The forest was vast and finding new homes was easy. Plus the sheriff's men couldn't find their way around the place if John or Nasir left patrins on the ground or tied to trees for them to follow. So, moving from base camp to base camp over the years, often reusing ones they'd abandoned before, was easy and also, Robin had to admit, part of the fun.

He could imagine the Sheriff berating Gisburne after yet another excursion into Sherwood had resulted in a lot of tired horses, wet soldiers and angry captains and ultimately an angrier Sheriff. Robin enjoyed thinking about Gisburne getting into hot water with the Sheriff.

He smiled at the thought just as a silhouette loomed over him, temporarily holding the rain off his face.

It was Marion.

He smiled. How could he do anything else – it was the most involuntary thing Robin's face ever did. The sight of her eyes, the smell of her hair, the brightness of her smile. All these things made Robin's heart sing.

'Would you be interested in some food?' she asked him. 'Much has rabbit and Nasir has returned with a deer.'

'That'll have the Sheriff even angrier than normal,' Robin laughed.

'I hope so,' agreed Marion. 'Well?'

'In a while,' he replied. 'Right now, I'm enjoying the peace and quiet of staring into the sky and daydreaming about... nothing.'

'Well don't drift away,' Marion said. 'Or Will and John will make sure there's nothing left at all.'

And she vanished from view.

He listened to her soft footfall as she moved back to the small fire – powerful enough to cook and warm them, not too large to produce smoke that could be seen more than a few feet away.

He slowly let the voices of the others: Much, John, Will, Tuck and even Nasir drifted in and out of focus.

And Robin closed his eyes. Just a few more moments, and then it would be warm venison for dinner...

***

Benjamin Hockleaf parted some bushes with his sword, as if expecting to find Robin Hood and his merry men hiding there, ready to be caught. He imagined they would throw their arms up while Sam bound them with rope. Benjamin and Sam would then lead them, at sword-point back to the castle. There, the Sheriff would knight them for their astounding work, while Sir Hiss sat in the corner, glowering at them.

Benjamin was brought metaphorically down to earth with a crash as Sam suddenly said into his ear 'What are we doing out here, Ben? We're not going to find outlaws in this part of Sherwood Forest.'

Benjamin shook his headband let out a deep sigh. 'I know these woods, lad. I know the twists and turns and dales and nooks. If anyone can find them, if anyone can read the broken twigs and bent grasses and disturbed ground, it's Benjamin Hockleaf, and don't you forget it.'

'How can I?' asked Sam, looking around a tree in mock astonishment at not finding Robin Hood there. 'You tell me, you tell anyone who'll listen, that fact daily.'

Benjamin sheathed his sword. ''Tis true, that's why.'

Sam rolled his eyes. 'What makes you such an expert then?'

Benjamin gestured around them.

'Used to play in these woods as a lad, Sam Tully. Born and brought up in the village...' Benjamin suddenly found himself shivering. Maybe it was the damp, getting under his leathers. 'Mind you, we were never allowed to go this far in.'

Sam giggled. 'Why not?'

'They used to tell us things… things about the heart of Sherwood Forest. Things to keep us away.'

'Us?'

Benjamin nodded. 'My friends. And…'

Sam's eyes sparkled. 'And? And who?'

'There was Robert Kirlings, there was Adam Bell, there was Peter Fayre and there was… there was Robin. Of Loxley.'

'Robin? As in Robin I'the Hood? The man we're chasing? You knew him?'

'Used to come out and play with the rest of the village young-uns.' Benjamin cleared his throat, as if coughing away the memories. 'We were only 8 or 9 summers back then.' He breathed in the misty air. 'A long time before the exile too.'

'Hold on a minute. What exile?'

Benjamin ignored him. 'So it stands to reason that if I know every hiding place in this part of Sherwood Forest, so will he. I know places to look the Sheriff and Gisburne have never even thought of.'

But Sam Tully wasn't letting the revelation go. 'No, wait a minute, back up a bit. What… exile?'

Benjamin sighed out a long, deep breath, remembering the past. Remembering a lifetime ago when everything was simple and innocent and fun.

'Well, Robin wasn't always an outlaw, you know. When I first knew him, he'd just been sent to the Miller's house after his parents died. Lord Ailric of Loxley and his lady wife, Maire.'

Sam was dumbfounded. This was new information. 'So, how'd he end up living in your village?'

Benjamin shrugged. 'I'm not sure – something to do with old Ailric and the Gisburnes not seeing eye to eye. I reckon he ended up with us to avoid him getting, you know…' and Benjamin drew his finger across his throat with an accompanying gurgling noise. 'Probably explains why Sir Hiss and the Sheriff can't bear him.'

Sam smiled and Benjamin realised he'd said the nickname out loud.

'Gisburne. Sir Guy. Sir Guy of Gisburne,' Benjamin said formally, is if saying it would automatically make all right with the world again.

But Sam wasn't letting go of any of this. 'So, how'd you get to know Robin's story so well?

Benjamin shivered again and instinctively looked deeper into the woodlands, through the ferns and trees. He was sure it was darker further ahead than it should have been. It felt… wrong. It felt almost unnatural in there.

He looked back at Sam, hoping that telling his story would shake off the feeling that they were being watched. That they were in…

He cleared his throat again. 'My old Da' worked for Lord Ailric, was one of his guards-at-arms. I would have probably ended up the same if Loxley Castle hadn't fallen.' Benjamin swallowed a crack in his voice. 'I never saw my Da' again after that. My ma always said he died along with Ailric.'

Sam nodded. 'I'm sorry to hear that, I am. That's like in my town when they took everyone off to the Holy Lands for Richard. I exact he's a headless corpse now, cut to bits by godless savages.'

Benjamin shook his head. 'You're a cheerful one, Sam Tully, no mistake.'

Benjamin was about to say something else when he stopped and held his arm out, pressing his palm against Sam's chest.

Sam knew well enough not to argue at that. Benjamin's age and experience meant that Sam wouldn't argue. He too froze.

After a moment, Benjamin relaxed and stepped into the bushes, Sam following silently a few paces behind.

Then Benjamin Hockleaf stopped dead in his tracks.

They were in a dense copse, the branches of the trees cutting out all light from the sky above, creating a thick dark circle. The darkness Benjamin had sensed earlier perhaps.

He drew his sword for at the centre of the darkness was a small hut. An old shack that was made from hundreds of twigs and branches, woven together by old cloth.

Logically, Benjamin thought one good gust of wind should bring it down.

But childhood stories and warnings told him however that this was a building nothing natural could destroy.

Because it itself was not natural.

It was dark, foreboding. It was…

'Evil,' Sam whispered from behind.

Sam Tully, who didn't have the stories in his head, didn't have the local knowledge or folklore, had put his finger right on it.

This place reeked of evil.

'What is it?' Sam asked, his voice suddenly betraying its youthfulness through its timidity.

Benjamin knew he had to be strong and sure for both of them. 'It's a hut. Might be what we're looking for.'

Sam was unconvinced. 'I dunno 'bout that. If that's an outlaws' den, well it's barely big enough for Robin Hood, let alone all his men too, isn't it?'

Benjamin Hockleaf took in a deep breath and pulled himself up to his full height. 'Let's find out, yes? Be good to report back something positive for change.' He turned and winked at Sam 'Might be enough to get me back on the horses.'

But Sam was clearly having none of it. He stepped backwards, crossing himself. 'There's something… wrong about this place,' he muttered.

Benjamin, who knew enough legends and stories about Sherwood Forest nevertheless also knew he had to push on. 'Look, Sam, it's just a hut. A shack. It's hardly the scariest building in the country, is it?'

'May I help you, gentlemen?'

Benjamin Hockleaf and Sam Tully had never moved faster in their lives.

Both had their swords drawn with a speed that Guy of Gisburne would have been proud of; the tips of each rested against the neck of the speaker behind them as the men spun around.

It was a scrawny neck those blade tips met as well, ribbed like a chicken's gullet, and it vibrated as the old woman who owned it swallowed in surprise.

She was a small woman, dressed in a black cloak, with a black hood overing much of her head.

Talon-like thin hands grabbed a staff in one hand, a basket in the other. Her skin was so thin that Benjamin could not just see the blue veins close to the surface but was convinced he could actually see movement as the blood moved through them.

She smiled a toothy grin, although a few teeth had long since decayed to dust. But as she did so, Benjamin was drawn to the eyes. If every other part of the woman before him suggested great age, an age that also suggested she probably ought to have been dead a good decade a two, her eyes told a wholly different story. They burned with life, with energy, with no bloodshot corners or cloudy eyes. Instead he felt that his heart was being turned to ice just by looking at the cold blueness that was staring back at him.

'Who are you?' Sam was asking. He was already lowering his sword, but Benjamin didn't.

The old woman's look flicked back and forth and finally settled on the sword at her throat.

She lifted her basket. In it were a few birds' eggs and some grasses. 'Just getting supplies for my supper,' she said. 'You going to tell Abbot Hugo? 'Tis only a few birdie eggs.'

'My friend asked you a question,' said Benjamin finally finding his voice after a second of two of dry throat. 'You gave us quite a surprise sneaking up behind us.'

The old woman shrugged but never took her eyes off Benjamin. She cocked her head slightly, as if trying to remember. A long bony finger unwrapped slowly from the staff she held and pointed at him.

'Yes Benjamin Hockleaf, I gave you a "surprise". But not a "fright" I'll warrant.'

'What do you mean, old woman?'

She gave a small cackle that made Benjamin shiver again, just as he had earlier when he sensed something dark at the heart of Sherwood Forest.

Sam took over the questioning.

'What are you doing here? Now?'

She never took her eyes of Benjamin as she answered Sam. 'Coming home of course. Listening to you two nattering on about Robin of Loxley.' She laughed again. 'The Hooded Man. Not found him yet then?'

'You live here?' Benjamin persisted.

'Oh I always have done Benjamin Hockleaf. Always.'

'How do you know me?'

The old woman smiled a rather rictus grin that again caused a shiver to run through Benjamin. 'Same as you know me.'

Sam found his voice.

'Answer his question, old woman, before I run you through.'

Finally, her eyes moved to stare at Sam, and he took an involuntary step backwards, his sword raised again.

'Thing is, I don't know you. Not sure I want to.' She stepped between them and instinctively they stepped aside to let her part them and walk towards the shack. 'Go away,' she said.

Benjamin reached out and grabbed her shoulder. 'Now listen…'

'With astonishing strength, she simply shrugged his grip away and turned to face them both, her eyes wider and more vibrant than ever.

'No, you listen spawn of Old Clem Hockleaf. Think – for once. Think back. Remember.' She waved her basket-carrying hand towards the surrounding copse. 'These woods. You. Adam. Robin. Much. The rest of you younglings. Being a child. The stories. Remember all the stories…'

And Benjamin could swear he heard voices. Children's voices. And then he could see, pushing through the woods, tiny figures running laughing and then stopping in shock as they encountered the shack. And the old woman. In black. With a basket and a staff. And the eyes. Eyes that bore into their eight-year-old souls.

But that was impossible because that had been twenty-five summers past at least. And she was old, decaying back then. But here, today, she hadn't changed in the slightest.

And just as had happened back then, the forest suddenly seemed smaller and darker and colder and full of monsters and demons and creatures whose only mission was to devour the hearts and souls of those children. And also him. Here today.

Benjamin looked around, and sure enough the darkness was present again, getting closer. He was sure there was sound too, a whispering sound like a hundred voices but each one from a hundred miles away and in his head at the same time.

'But… but this is impossible…' Benjamin managed to mutter. He turned to say something to Sam.

But Sam was gone. He couldn't have moved away, Benjamin would have seen him, but he was no longer there.

'Sam? Sam?' He growled at the old woman, who was still grinning like a mad thing. And, if possible, her skin seemed to have stretched even tighter and thinner across her face, the grin looking increasingly like some demonic vision of death.

'Where is Sam? Where is he?'

And the noise and the darkness and the visions and everything was gone as suddenly as it had arrived.

Benjamin could feel his heart racing. He jabbed his sword towards the old woman but she swung her staff expertly and the sword went flying off to the right, disappearing into the bushes.

And Benjamin realised he couldn't move. Was it fear rooting him to the spot, or was it something else?

'Where's Sam Tully?' In his head, he was yelling, but in his ears, he knew it had come out as little more than a whimper – the kind a dog gives before it knows it is going to whipped for the hundredth time.

'Gone. Won't be back,' was all she replied.

Benjamin wanted to know what that meant. Gone? Gone where?

And as if she could read his paralysed mind, the old woman lent forward. He could feel her foul breath on his lips, she was that close.

'Oh, you remember the stories, Ben. You know where he's gone, don't you…'

Benjamin wanted to scream, wanted to run away, wanted to strangle her, wanted to do a hundred things that he realised he couldn't. Because he couldn't move. The only thing he felt was panic, rising up through his stomach, his breast, into his throat.

It couldn't be true. How could it? The village elders always said not to come here, but that was just to scare them as children. It wasn't *true*. The Evil

Woman of the Forest, The Scavenger, the Harpy, the Old Witch… they were just stories.

And yet here she was. Exactly as he and the others had seen her all those years ago.

Looking the same.

Giving him the same fetid stare, just as she had done then.

Benjamin finally managed to expel one long breath, as if it has been drawn out of his body.

And as his eyes burned with tears that would not fall to his cheek, he realised that the old woman was breathing in as he breathed out, as if she was feeding off his last, dying breath…

CHAPTER TWO

The alchemists and potion-makers would always tell you that the easiest way to evoke a strong memory is not through the sense of sight or touch but smell. Aromas trigger responses, fears, nostalgia and above all, passions.

If that were true, and Robin had no reason to doubt those learned men and teachers, then the smells drifting into his nose were warm, comforting and above all, relaxing.

A variety of roast meats and vegetables, fruits and sweetmeats, mead and wine, all combining together in the air with the added tartness of the oil flambeaux and charred cedarwood that pervaded Loxley Castle.

Robin was seated alone, on a set of winding steps that led up to a turret behind him and down to the main dining hall below.

He was watching the meal in progress, a grin across his face as he watched his friends and family having what he could only describe as a good time.

And there, seated at the head of the table were his parents, Lord Ailric and the lady Maire. And at the right hand of his father was Robin's new bride, Marion of Leaford and next to her, roaring his head off at some biting remark made by some other nobleman, was Marion's own father, Richard.

Robin breathed the fumes in once more and then got up off the steps and walked down towards the feast.

'Ho, my Lord Ailric,' Richard of Leaford said, 'my son-in-law finally deigns to join us.'

Robin mock bowed to Richard. 'My Lord, I did not wish to upstage your rare presence at our table, so I thought it best to delay my arrival until after you were sated upon my father's venison and beef. So that I, should you challenge me to a drunken duel, would be able to move that much faster than you.'

Robin walked behind his wife, running his hand through her hair. She snatched at his hand as he finished, kissed the back of it and then held him in place, forbidding any further steps away from her.

Richard was howling with laughter at Robin's jest, as was the Lady Maire.

But Robin realised that the smile formed on his father's mouth did not reach his eyes and Robin raised a quizzical eyebrow.

Lord Ailric waved his son over and with a returned kiss to the back of Marion's hand, Robin eased from her side and went around to stand between his mother and father.

'Your father is upset,' Maire whispered.

'Indeed?'

'I sent word to the Prince of our feast.'

'You expected him to come?'

Ailric shook his head. 'Of course not, but I would have expected a response of some sort, an acknowledgement. Possibly a substitute.'

'I shouldn't worry, Father. I'm sure the Prince has what he perceives as better things to do than support a loyal nobleman.' Robin leaned closer. 'He's probably slaughtering some peasants near Newark or something equally vile that he considers sport.'

The lady Maire threw a glance at Richard of Leaford then back at her son. 'Hush.'

Robin shrugged. "Mother, the man is a monster. The sooner King Richard returns and consigns John to a tarpit somewhere, the better for England.'

Lord Ailric was concerned more with aspects of the Prince closer to home. 'I suspect we have fallen out of favour, Robin. It may be that I need to send you to greet him at Newark, build some bridges.'

'Me, Father? Build bridges with John?'

'Prince John,' corrected Lady Maire.

This last reference had been louder than she had intended and Richard of Leaford's ears pricked up.

'You speak of my friend the Prince? Is there anything I can help you with, friend Thane?'

Lord Ailric shook his head, forcing that grin a bit wider. 'No, it is—'

'Rude,' Robin finished for him, causing Ailric's eyes to widen in shock. 'My father invited your Prince John to this feast and yet he could not bring himself to respond with even the courtesy of a polite refusal.'

Richard shrugged. 'The Prince is a great man, with many callers upon his time. I should not take it personally,' Richard said, smiling at his daughter. 'Mayhaps you should consider my presence here not just as father of the bride but as a representative of Nottingham Castle and its environs.' Then he added with just a hint of steel. 'And of my friend and benefactor, the Prince himself.'

Robin tensed as if to retort, but Lady Maire grasped his wrist and squeezed. Tightly. Robin gave her a look and then then took a deep breath.

'What is your vexation with Prince John?' Richard continued.

Marion in turn took her father's hand. 'Father, I'm sure it is nothing. Let us try some of these fine tubers and sweetmeats, yes?'

But Richard snatched his hand back. 'I ask again my Lords Ailric and Robin, what are your concerns about the Regent of our lands?'

Marion leaned closer to her hosts, deliberately blocking her father's view of them, partially at least.

'My Lord Loxley, thank you. And thank you, Lady Maire, for this glorious feast.'

Lady Maire took the opportunity that Marion had so wisely engineered. 'No feast is too much for the Lady who has joined our family this day.' The lady Maire threw a look towards Robin. 'You have made our son so happy.'

'I am very glad to hear it,' Marion replied and eased Robin into a seat fully satisfied that she and her mother-in-law had diffused the situation.

Lady Maire continued 'Your father seems greatly relaxed now he is home from the Crusades.'

As if the irony of that comment wasn't enough, Richard chose that exact moment to slide his seat noisily back across the stone floor and stand, eyes blazing in anger towards Robin.

Robin stared back, a slight suggestion of an expression that said, "shall we take this outside?" on his face.

Richard ignored his daughter's outstretched hand as he squared up to Robin. 'Mayhaps my daughter's choice has not been as good as I believed,' he said waspishly.

Robin said nothing, but now there was just a hint of amusement on his lips.

'My lords,' Lord Ailric started. 'My friends…' But neither were listening.

'My Lady Marion?' A soft voice from across the table spoke.

Marion nodded to the speaker. 'Lord Ailric, my Lady Maire… Have you met my good friend and teacher, the Friar, Tuck?'

'A pleasure, good friar,' smiled Lady Maire although her eyes were flicking back and forth towards Robin as he and Richard had walked towards the far end of the Hall.

'My Lady,' said Tuck. 'My good Lord,' he addressed Lord Ailric. Then without awaiting a response, he smiled over the smouldering meats at Marion.

'Marion, I fear your new husband and your father seem to be getting into a rather intractable argument about the… benefits of Prince John. I suspect your calming influence over both may be required.'

Marion nodded. 'Of course.' She nodded to her hosts as she eased her chair back, far less noisily than her father had. 'If you will excuse me.'

'But of course, my dear,' said Lord Ailric in a weary voice, that suggested he was well-versed in Robin arguing with dinner guests.

At which point a massive cheer went up from a newly gathered group behind them; they all turned to see Robin flat on his backside and Marion's father ready to strike again should Robin be foolish enough to stand up to him once more.

Marion sighed loudly and tossed a look towards Tuck. 'Oh dear, the argument appears to be over and I fear my husband has lost to my father.'

Tuck rose too. 'Let's go and calm the situation down.'

The two friends walked towards the cheering crowd, although its raucous noise petered out as they did so.

Angrily, Richard glanced at his daughter, said nothing but turned on his heel and headed back towards his hosts and the feast.

Robin was being helped up by one of the guards. 'Thank you, Ben,' he muttered, then caught a look from his new wife. 'What?' he protested as innocently as he could muster. 'Marion?'

'Dearest.'

'Your father—'

Marion spoke to Robin as she would a six-year-old with a bloody nose. '—is an old man, with old man's views. And you should not let him concern you so.'

'But he's such a—'

'An old friend of your family,' Friar Tuck offered up. 'And especially your father.'

Robin took a breath, knowing he was in the wrong but determined to get the last word. 'Just because they fought together against Saladin's armies—'

With a well-practised indication of times to come, Marion put a finger on Robin's lips. 'Hush my love. Be calm. Let us not spoil this wonderful night of celebration your parents have set up.'

Robin looked into his wife's beautiful eyes and his shoulders sagged. 'If you say so.'

'I do.'

'You…' Robin began. 'You are amazing, and I am so lucky to have you as my wife.'

Marion snorted slightly and leaned closer. 'Actually, I think you'll find you are *my* husband.'

Robin's mouth dropped open in mock horror. 'Now then—'

And Tuck's arm fell on his shoulder. 'Oh no, Robin my friend. I wouldn't argue with Marion on that. She can be very wilful.'

Marion now raised an eyebrow in his direction. 'I can hear you most clearly, Tuck.'

Friar Tuck chortled. 'You were meant to.' He gently turned their heads back in the other direction. 'Oh look, I do believe John Little and his lovely Meg are about to start dancing to the players' tunes. You should join them.'

Robin nodded and started back, and as Marion followed, she took Tuck's hand. 'Thank you.'

Marian called back to those who had watched the altercation. 'Come my friends, let us indeed dance.'

And she realised something was amiss. Instead of moving towards the party, Robin had stopped dead in the middle of the hall.

'Robin?' Marion said.

Robin was starting at the staircase he has descended from earlier, the one that led only up to an old tower room. 'Did you see her?'

'See who, my husband?'

'The woman. In green.'

'One of the servants?'

'No.' Robin wasn't sure how he knew that for certain, but certain he was. 'I know all the servants. And why has she gone up there.'

'It matters not,' Marion said.

But Robin cut across her. 'You go dance. I shall join you shortly.'

Marion laughed. 'I am now most intrigued. Who is this lady who can steal a husband from his bride on the afternoon of their wedding?'

But Robin was no longer listening. In his head, the sounds of music, of dancing, laughter and cheers were starting to fade. As if he were many yards from the Hall. Even Marion's voice was lost in the hugger-mugger that was rapidly becoming no more than a hint of a murmur at the back of his mind.

And the world was silent except for his footsteps on the stone steps as he ascended towards the tower rooms.

And just ahead of him, always out of reach, was the green-clad woman, her head hidden beneath the hood of her cape.

She turned the endless corner of the tower and Robin strode faster, surely but one footstep away now. But she was never ahead of him.

It was impossible.

'Where are you?' he muttered.

'Behind you, Robin of Loxley.'

Robin swung round and stared at the impossibility of a figure who had been steps ahead and was now as many behind.

'Who are you?' Robin asked. Although something that made his chest tighten and his heart grow cold told him that whatever answer she gave, would make little difference.

'This talk has been a long time coming,' the strange woman said with a smile. Robin could see the expression. But he could see nothing else of her face, just hear her strange voice… it seemed Celtic in origin. Welsh? Scots? Cornish, mayhaps? He couldn't quite place it. It was quiet, calm, but it had an authority he had not expected.

She pointed backwards, indicating the steps below which led towards the great hall. 'What is occurring back down there?'

Robin wasn't sure whether to engage with her or lop her head off. He was also surprised that such a visceral reaction could be occasioned towards someone he knew not. 'I asked who you are.'

'Explanations will have to wait. Tell me of the feast.'

'What of it?'

The Woman in Green shrugged. 'Celebrating the return of parents from the wars. Heroes, I am sure.'

Robin nodded. 'My father served his King well.'

The Woman in Green lowered her head, guaranteeing Robin could not see so much as a hint of skin. For a moment he wondered if under the hood, in the darkness, there was nothing but the smile he'd glimpsed earlier. But that was madness. She was just a woman.

Surely…

Her hooded head was now cocked to one side, as if daring him to look elsewhere and give her an opportunity to do… something. Although Robin could not imagine what.

'You must be pleased to have Ailric home,' she continued. 'In time for your wedding to the lady Marion. I see her own father has returned as well. King Richard looked after his people well, it would appear.'

Robin opened his mouth to say something, but no words came out. He simply didn't understand who this woman was. And yet she seemed terribly familiar, something on the tip of his memory, something he felt he knew from a story—

The Woman in Green suddenly grabbed his wrist, and he didn't shake her off. Instead, he looked at the hand, but it seemed… blurred almost. He couldn't tell if it was the hand of a crone, a maiden or anything at all. In his eyes it was just… a hand. But there was something unusual about it. Yes of course. But surely that can't be right, no one has—

'Oh, you are thinking too hard about today, young Robin. Turn your thoughts elsewhere.'

Shaken from the reverie, Robin took a deep breath.

'I should return to my wife, to my guests…'

But the Woman in Green shook her head slowly. It was a movement of neither sorrow nor command, but of something… malevolent. Almost bird-like…

'No, Robin, let's not!'

***

Robin sat upright with a gasp.

There was air on his face, and a slight damp within that air. He sniffed and smelled… freshness, cleanliness. Everything that wasn't the inside of the castle.

He opened his eyes, blinking away the sudden, different light. A group of people stared at him, men in ill-fitting dirty clothes, some carrying swords, knives, bows…

His own clothes had lost their finery. Instead, he was in woollens and leather. Trousers hewn from rough cloth, boots from -

'Robin, we were wondering when you were going to wake up! The weather has turned against us, it seems.'

Robin didn't know this man at all, but surely over there, pouring hot water over some vegetables… was that John Little? But he'd been with Robin, back in the Great Hall… seconds ago…

Another voice spoke, this one to his right. Robin turned to face the grinning face of the man who proffered a hand to help Robin rise. Automatically, Robin accepted the aid.

'We're making the most of the meats you got from under the Sheriff's nose. You should have some of this.'

Robin realised who this was too. 'Friar Tuck? What… where is this?'

The man who had first spoken to him frowned.

'Robin? Are you all right?'

Robin tried to clear his head. The Great Hall. His wedding. The Woman in Green on the stairwell…

'How did I get here?'

'Tuck, is he all right?' Will Scarlet asked, tapping his temple meaningfully.

Friar Tuck put the back of his hand to Robin's forehead; Robin was too bewildered to move away.

'No fever as far as I can tell, Will,' Tuck responded.

Robin looked around. 'Is this Sherwood?'

'Where else would we be?'

A woman's voice spoke – one he knew instantly – and the men eased apart as she strode between them towards him.

'Marion?'

Then there was another voice, but this one wasn't from anyone present. It was in his ear. Or in his head. Or both.

'Ignore this rabble, Robin of Loxley. It is too soon…'

Robin recognised the unplaceable accent of the Woman in Green. But where was she? How could he hear her but not see her?

Then his attention snapped back to Marion.

'Marion? My wife… out here… with this… rabble?'

John Little frowned. 'Rabble?'

But it was Marion's simple enquiry that shook Robin the most.

'Wife?'

Before he could say anything in return, Friar Tuck was calling to the other men.

'You hear that Much? Nasir? Robin thinks us all a rabble nowadays!'

John Little suddenly roared with laughter. A man little more than a boy, face caked in mud and unkempt wispy hair, pushed passed him. 'Ha! That's wiped the evergreen smile from Much's face,' he chortled.

Then that peculiar voice in his head.

'But where are your parents, Robin of Loxley?'

Automatically, Robin repeated the question, hoping against hope that some light would be shed upon this waking nightmare. 'Where are my parents?'

Marion and the men all shared a look, each of them stopping whatever they were doing, then frowning at him. Marion walked to him and took both his hands in hers. Her lovely, soft, delicate hands. He looked down at them. They weren't as soft as he remembered, as if she had spent many months or years working. They still bore skin that he recognised and which excited him at the slightest brush, but her fingers were calloused, streaked with dirt.

'Your parents?' she said quietly. 'But Robin, they have been—'

***

Robin sat upright with a gasp.

There was air on his face, and a slight mustiness within that air. He sniffed and smelled… smoke, sweetmeats and… something else, clawing at his throat. Everything that wasn't the outside of Sherwood Forest.

He was back on the stairwell but sitting now. He didn't remember sitting, no, he remembered…

'Marion…'

He remembered the woods, and John Little and that fat Friar friend of Marion's and—

'What was that?' he snapped at the Woman in Green, her head still hidden. 'A vision? A nightmare?'

'Do you have nightmares?' she asked.

'Who are you?'

The Woman in Green took a step backwards down towards the Great Hall.

'The bigger question is who are you? Are you Robin of Loxley, son of Ailric and Maire? Or Robin, son of the Miller? Are you perhaps Robin, Hooded Man of the Forest?'

Robin stared at the vision in front of him, his mind replaying that moment when he had felt her hand on his wrist, seen that strange…

'Which is it to be?' she snapped.

But before he could say another word, a piercing scream came from below. One word. Screamed by his beloved new wife.

'Robin!'

CHAPTER THREE

Robin had no idea if he had pushed past the Woman in Green or pushed her ahead of him. Or if she had tumbled or simply vanished into thin air.

He only remembered the sight he saw at the foot of the stairwell as he arrived back in the Great Hall of Loxley Castle.

He knew. He'd known from the moment he'd awoken on that stairwell. That strange smell that had greeted his nostrils that had been clawing at the back of his throat and nose.

It was the smell of death.

And it was prevalent throughout the Great Hall.

He crossed the room in two steps and scooped Marion up in his arms.

For a brief second, her eyes fluttered and opened, seeming to glisten, acknowledging that the pained, awful scream had succeeded in bringing him back to her side.

But far too late.

He felt the breath on his face as she died, felt the energy drain from her, almost a physical feeling as if her life were draining from her head to her feet in seconds. Where once he had held, danced with, kissed and embraced the most beautiful woman in the world, he now only held a physical being with her aspect.

Her being, her soul, everything that made Marion who she was, had gone. Forever.

He didn't try to stop the tears that rolled down his face as he buried her head against his neck. But he stared through salted eyes at the others around the table. Around the entire Hall.

Lords. Ladies. Friends. Servants. Guards.

All were slumped in their seats or collapsed on the floor where they had been standing.

Where but a few moments ago this had been a room of unbridled joy and love, it was now a cold tomb denied anything other than misery.

After a few moments, or perhaps many hours, Robin neither knew not cared, he finally eased Marion's body back into her seat.

Wiping his face, he took in her father, Richard of Leaford, sat alongside Robin's own father Ailric of Loxley. Opposite was the fat Friar, Tuck. At the far end, John and Meg Little. Between them, names and faces Robin had known for many years or just a few hours.

All dead.

All died in pain.

He glanced to the servants and guards. They too seemed to have died grimacing.

Had no one tried to defend their lords? Had no one attempted even to flee, to call for aid.

'There are no marks on their bodies,' said the Woman in Green who was suddenly at Robin's side.

'What... has happened?' Robin's voice was a hoarse whisper, such was his grief. 'What have you done?'

'I have done nothing.'

'Marion. My wife. My family. My friends... This cannot be happening.'

'If it helps you, Robin. I can assure you, it is not.'

'What isn't?' Robin placed a hand on his father's face, closing his eyes.

The Woman in Green waved her arm around the room. 'This. Any of it. But I know it feels real at the moment.' She took a step towards Robin, then stopped. He had scooped up a knife from the pig on the table. It may not have been a warrior's knife, but it was sharp, dangerous and would do the job perfectly. With a slight slump, the Woman in Green finally drew her hood back and it fell away and for the first time Robin could see who he was talking to.

Except he couldn't. Perhaps it was the shock, or the grief, or the anger. But no matter how hard he stared, Robin could not focus on her face. It seemed to be ever-changing. Was she young? Was she old? Was she tall, short? Like her accent beforehand, something was preventing Robin from focusing and identifying the most basic facets of what he was seeing.

The only thing he was sure of was that her hair, long and waved, hung down her back and was the same shade of green as her cloak.

Green like leaves on the trees, like the grass of Sherwood Forest.

That was what he had sensed earlier when she had held his wrist, the thing he had been unable to realise. Her skin had possessed the same slightly green hue, as if green blood flowed through her veins rather than red, lending her flesh a slightly olive tone.

And whilst he still could not perceive her features through his vale of confusion, he realised that she was no longer wearing the cloak. Instead, it seemed to move by itself and reshape around her body, forming a long green dress that hung but a fraction higher than her feet, held at the waist by a green belt that, if he didn't know better, seemed to be made from long thin twigs from a willow tree.

'I need you to move away from Marion, Robin. Think. You are being deceived.

Robin nodded. 'By you…'

'No, not by me. Please, leave Marion, leave your beloved father too and come, stand by me.'

Not sure why, Robin did so. She motioned for him to look once again at the ghastly tableaux before them.

'Look beyond your grief. Look at the people at this table. In this Hall.'

'What of them? They are dead.'

'How?' The Woman in Green pointed at them all. 'As I said, no marks.'

'Poisoned. The food… You! You kept me away from this. Why?'

But the Woman in Green ignored his question, instead asking another of her own. 'How many people are here, Robin? I count thirty-seven bodies. Every guest, servant, guard and minstrel, dead.'

'And?'

'There were thirty-nine people at this feast. And if you were the thirty-eighth..?'

Her words were interrupted by a guttural growl from the far side of the Great hall. Near the doorway.

'My Lord… of… Loxley…'

Robin was immediately focused on who had uttered the words.

'A guardsman. He lives!'

Robin was at his side in a breath, the Woman in Green there too, almost unnaturally, as if walking weren't something she had to do. She was just… there.

But that was of no interest to Robin now. 'Speak good fellow… what did you witness?'

The man was in great pain – Robin could only imagine the huge feat of strength and bravery it took to fight through the pain of the poison.

He managed one word before coughing blood. 'Darkness…'

Robin gently patted his face. 'Stay awake, friend. What is your name? Tell me your name...'

The man looked up at his master, eyes watering.

'Ben, sir. Benjamin Hockleaf. It was the Dragons. The spirits of the ancient ones...'

Robin threw a look over to the Woman in Green. 'I don't understand?'

Benjamin's body shuddered. 'Tracing the lines... they came... tracing the lines to the past and future. The Dragons. Converging... at the Point of Power.' And then one final bewildering thing occurred. Although Benjamin Hockleaf's lips moved, the voice that came from the throat was not his. It was that of a woman. Old, cracked. Wracked with sibilance and bitterness. 'Find them. Find me.'

And Benjamin died, like Marion before him, in Robin's arms.

'Dead,' Robin muttered. 'Like all the others.'

'Except the missing one,' said the Woman in Green.

Robin again tried to focus on her face, but again to no avail.

'Did you hear his last words?'

The Woman in Green shook her head. 'They were not his words.'

'Whose?'

'The one who is not here.'

Robin stood up angrily, finally at the end of his tether. 'Stop speaking in riddles. Show me your face and tell me who you are.'

Almost imperceptibly, the Woman in Green took a step back.

And her face was clear.

Despite his grief, despite his anger and bewilderment, Robin had to acknowledge, she was beautiful. The kind of beauty that women the country overstrode to achieve, but even Marion could never entirely manage. It was as if this woman was quite simply perfect, as if every kind of beauty imaginable was captured in her features. Was she old, was she young? She was neither and yet both. She was ageless.

'What is your name?' Robin finally was able to say.

'I am usually spoken of as the Dodwoman. I have no other name.' Then she smiled. 'Well, that is not true. Many have given me names, but none are as true as Dodwoman.'

'I did not see you at the feast. How do I know you didn't do this, despite your protestations?'

'You don't. You must just accept that until you saw me at the foot of the stairwell, I was not here. Had I been, I doubt I could have stopped this. Not that it matters.

'Matters? Of course it matters, my wife, my parents, my friends are all dead.'

'It doesn't matter, Robin of Loxley, because this is but a phantom life, conjured to lure you into a trap. I had to come here to help you side-step it. But I was too late. Again,' she added firmly, 'I ask you to tell me who isn't here. One is missing and I fear you have overlooked them in your grief. For you have already assumed they are dead, but there is no body. Someone is missing.'

Frustrated and not understanding, Robin's eyes scoured the room.

And then he realised. With a sickness in the pit of his stomach, he saw the space at the table.

'I was sure... I was convinced...'

'Who is missing?'

'My mother. The Lady Maire.' He turned to the Dodwoman. 'Where is she?'

'She, like all of these people was not really here. This is but a dream. A nightmare I believe you called it. A trap that has now been sprung for you. Having walked into it, therefore, we must explore it if we are to ever find a way home.'

'I don't understand a word of this.'

The Dodwoman pointed to the dead guard who had warned them in both his own voice and that of another.

'Do you recognise him?'

'He said his name was—'

'No,' interrupted the Dodwoman. 'I said do you recognise him?'

'No. I have never seen Ben before.'

'Yes, you have. You grew up alongside him. He was one of your earliest friends until circumstances and allegiances pulled you slowly apart. His presence here, him being used as the instrument of information is her way of toying with us. Offering you tiny morsels.' The Dodwoman shook her head. 'Oh but she is still as clever and malicious as ever.

'Who? My mother?'

'Robin, your mother died many years ago. The Lady Maire you saw here today, along with Marion, Ailric, all of them are ghosts of your past being used against you.'

'But Marion...'

'That was the cruellest trick of all. Giving you your heart's desire to throw you off balance.'

'Robin?'

Robin swung around.

24

The Dodwoman frowned. 'What's wrong?'

'Did you nor hear that? Someone said my name.'

'Robin.'

'There! Again!' Robin looked back at the Dodwoman. 'It must be you. Bewitching me. Making me hear strange voices.'

'Your false mother perhaps?'

'No, the voice was male. But far away.'

'Ha,' the Dodwoman laughed suddenly. 'Now he chooses to show his hand. To become involved.'

'Robin. Find me.'

The Dodwoman smiled. 'He spoke again, yes?'

'So you can hear him.'

She shook her head. 'Not yet. He and I exist on the same plane, but in this dreamscape, he cannot reach me. Only his champion.'

'Robin. The thing you believe to be your mother. She is the key. Focus upon her. Bring her to you. To us.'

'What's he saying?' asked the Dodwoman. 'He had best not be blaming me for all this. Again.'

'Robin, focus...'

The Dodwoman carried on. 'Mind you, together he and I need to keep this dreamland of "never was" and "might have been" breathing.'

Robin threw her a look of pure venom.

The Dodwoman sighed. 'Robin, trust me, I am here to help. So is the voice you can hear. In his own peculiar way. I am ancient but I am also the here and now. I am here to save you.'

'As you saved my wife? My family and friends?'

'They did not need saving. They do not exist.'

'You are speaking in riddles.'

The male voice in his head spoke.

'You are a hero, Robin.'

The Dodwoman spoke at the same time. 'You are a hero, Robin.'

Robin was getting angrier than ever. Surely, he was mad. It was the only explanation he could give himself.

The Dodwoman carried on, as if utterly unaware of his distress.

'To the people we briefly encountered outside. To the inhabitants of Nottingham, of England. And especially to the spirits of this land, you are a hero. I am here to take you back to them. For you have become... lost.

Robin reached once again toward the table, toward the carving knife. 'Why?' he asked her.

'That is my purpose in life. I map the lines, illuminate the paths.'

'I don't know what you are talking about. I am no hero. I am Robin of Loxley, proud son of Ail...' His voice began to choke, so he cleared it. 'Of Ailric and Maire. Widower of fair Marion. And you... you speak of heroes, spirits and—'

In his head, the male voice suddenly bellowed, and Robin forgot the knife and put his hands to his head in sudden pain.

'Robin. I command you! Listen!'

Robin almost shrieked with the stabbing pain. 'Get out of my head, Demon voice!' Then he straightened up, determined to ignore the pain and focus on what really mattered. 'Or is it a Dragon Voice? Yes! One of those of which Benjamin Hockleaf forewarned me?'

The Dodwoman sighed loudly, as if she were suddenly irritated at having to talk to Robin is though he was but ten years old.

'No, Robin I'the Hood,' she said slowly. 'That voice is Herne the Hunter. And he needs you. Now!'

CHAPTER FOUR

R obin sat upright with a gasp.
There was air on his face, and a slight damp within that air. He sniffed and smelled… insects, spiders. Everything that wasn't the inside of the castle or Sherwood Forest.

For a half second, it went through his mind that it could be the result of a potion someone had slipped him. Perhaps it was something in the meat? Was it something as simple as him partaking of too much mead the night before alongside Will Scarlet?

Because Robin could not imagine any other reason for the visions that he was having. That he was married to Marion. That his family and friends had been murdered by his mother. That he couldn't even recall his life in Sherwood Forest.

Much of the latter had come back to him now – so presumably it had been a fever-induced dream.

Instead, he was feeling the rain slowly dripping from the leaves of the tall trees of Sherwood, smacking against his face, and waking him from these mares of death, betrayal and mistrustful women in green.

'Marion?' He had heard the sound from his own mouth and had eagerly awaited her soft, slightly mocking reply. 'Robin, you were drunk and for that you will surely suffer today.'

But Marion had not replied. And the ground beneath him hadn't been soft earth and damp ferns.

So, his eyes had shot open as he had sat upright.

Robin was in a cave; the water dripping on his face had come from smooth blobs forming the roof. Beneath him, rounded, damp rocks, each the size of two men.

He had been in caves before, but none as large as this. None with the steady blueish light that seemed to come from nowhere and everywhere at the same time.

And none as vast and never ending.

He got to his feet, warily making sure he didn't slide on the treacherous rocks. 'Where have you brought me now, Dodwoman?' he muttered darkly. 'These visions of yours are beginning to annoy me.'

But there came no reply.

'Woman, where are you?' he yelled, hearing his voice echo, demonstrating just how big this cavern really was. 'Woman?' he yelled louder, listening to his voice bounce back. He had no truthful way of working it out. All he knew was that the cavern was huge, with no obvious exit or ending. Yet there was air and the strange blueish light that reminded him of magical summer evenings with Marion on the banks of the Maun.

Robin knew that one did not just magically appear in strange caves, so that this was one of the Dodwoman's visions was in no doubt.

But why this? And where was she?

There was a sound behind him, and he swung round.

Nothing.

'Who's there?' he said, hotly.

'Robin?'

That was not Herne. Nor the Dodwoman. That voice was softer yet more imperious, strong but feminine.

'My son? Is that you?'

'Mother?'

And there before him, stepping out of a shadow that hadn't been a shadow a moment earlier, was Lady Maire, wife of Ailric of Loxley, mother to Robin.

'Mother?' Robin felt as if someone had punched him in the gut. To have dreamed she had been alive at his wedding was one thing but knowing that was a vision was another. With that information in his mind, seeing her clearly here for the first time since he had been a boy – that was a pain, an anguish he had no idea he could experience. Nor know how to deal with.

'How is this possible?' he finally managed to find his voice to address her. To address his...

'Mother, you are dead.'

Words no one should have had to say to anyone. Least of all someone for whom he had grieved many years previously, whose memory he had locked away in his head and heart, assuming he would never see her beautiful face again.

'This is wrong.'

Lady Maire took a step towards him, and he instinctively looked to her feet, to ensure she didn't slip.

But of course, she didn't, she walked with an ease and a surety that further told him this could not be real.

'What are you saying, my son?'

Even though the words caught in his throat, Robin managed to say 'Mother, you are dead.'

That punch to the gut again. This just wasn't fair.

'What are you saying, my son?'

'Look me in the eye, Mother, tell me that this is really you.'

The Lady Maire just turned her head downwards, then her eyes flashed up, hooded, to stare at him.

He had forgotten just how beautiful she was. Her hazel eyes flecked with black, her freckled face and russet hair—

Wait! His mother had long dark hair, the colour of heartwood, like his own.

Red hair, freckles, hazel eyes – that was Marion!

Despite his confusion, he found a smile growing on his lips. Whoever his enemy was – and by now he was certain an enemy was at the heart of this – he had to admire them. They knew how to toy with him.

Sure enough, Lady Maire now had long dark hair rolling down her back, angelic Irish blue eyes twinkling in the cavern's gleaming. Exactly as he pictured her in his mind's eye whenever he brought her back to his mind.

'If you are really my mother, come face me. Let me see you eye to eye.' He pointed at the ground by his feet. 'Here.'

The Lady Maire let her eyes drop to her own feet again, refusing to move or match his angry gaze. 'Your father did all this, Robin. Ailric is at fault, do not chastise me, your poor lost mother.'

Robin didn't know whether to laugh at her audacity or weep at the fact that this vision of his beloved mother could be so warped and twisted.

But before he could speak, he heard a distant cry, ethereal however, rather than just a long way off.

It was male voice.

'Robin? Robin, where are you?'

'Ignore them, my son.'

Robin looked at his mother. 'Them? I only heard one voice calling.'

'Phantoms, sent to confuse you, to cloud your mind.'

'You seem very keen to make me think they are the phantoms, rather than yourself.'

29

'Robin?' A different voice.

And Robin knew that second voice, which made identifying the first obvious.

'John. And Tuck.'

'They are not here with us,' Lady Maire insisted.

'Obviously,' Robin retorted. 'But you weren't expecting them, otherwise you would have blocked me from hearing them, here in whatever hell you have brought me to.'

'You are confused, my poor son.'

And Robin finally let himself laugh. It wasn't a happy laugh, but one of harsh relief. 'Whoever you are, false Mother, I'm not confused.' And he took a deep breath and then bellowed towards the roof of the cavern. 'John! Tuck! Where are you?'

***

'It's stopped raining,' John Little said staring up at the sky.

'Thank you for that keen observation,' grunted Friar Tuck, as he parted a small bush of ferns aside.

John gave his companion a harsh look. The sort of look Tuck should have been grateful he didn't actually see.

'At least I'm not wasting time looking for Robin behind leaves that wouldn't come above his ankles.'

'He might be lying unconscious,' Tuck replied, 'Marion asked us to leave no stone – or fern – unturned.'

John shrugged. He knew Tuck was probably right, but they had been searching for Robin for many hours now and the light was fading. It was unlike Robin to simply wander off, but after his strange behaviour earlier, Marion had been right to be concerned.

So, Will and Marion had gone one way, Much and Nasir another – John imagined that if his and Tuck's conversations were getting needling, Nasir and poor Much would barely have anything to say to one another – whilst Tuck and John had taken the path that most directly led towards the heart of Sherwood Forest.

John pushed aside a particular thick undergrowth.

'Why do you think he'd be around here?' Tuck asked him.

'Because we've looked everywhere else.'

Friar Tuck shrugged. 'Sherwood Forest is a big place, John. You can't really say we've looked everywhere else.'

John sighed. Say nothing… say nothing… say—

'When did you start being so... annoying?' he snapped at the little priest.

Tuck looked like he'd been slapped with a particularly wet lettuce. 'I'm just saying...'

John cut across him by letting out a huge bellow as only a man of his size could. 'Robin?! Robin, where are you?'

Tuck shook his head in bewilderment and held his hands out wide in equal astonishment.

'Because that won't bring the Sheriff's men down on our heads,' he said to John.

John pursed his lips. 'Sherwood Forest's a big place, Tuck – remember?'

'Oh ha ha.'

John looked up a rather large tree. 'Besides, you know as well as I do, we can easily outwit the Sheriff's men in here.'

Friar Tuck shook his head as he continued searching for Robin. 'John, I'm just saying one day there will be more of them than we anticipate and then, well, our gooses will be cooked.'

'Well, I'm not giving up yet. Robin can't be far away – but if he's unconscious or worse, we need to find him.'

'I'm just saying—'

John stared down at Tuck, fire in his eyes. 'If you just say "I'm just saying" once more, Robin won't be the only "unconscious or worse" one missing tonight.'

Tuck stood, as if thinking about this. Then with a smile, he patted John's forearm. 'You make a compelling argument, my friend.' And then he hollered as loudly as he could. 'Robin!'

***

Back in the cavern, or whatever nightmare realm he was really in, Robin was making his way across the perilous rocks as he tried to work out from where he had heard Tuck and John's voices.

'Be careful, my son,' said Lady Maire's voice from behind. 'Those rocks are damp and slippery and—'

'I'm not your son. Or at least, you are not my mother.' Then more quietly, just to himself, he added 'Not really.'

'And yet, in your heart, you know I am.'

Robin finally turned back to state at... whatever she... it... was.

'In my heart, all I know is that you want me to think that.'

'Why?'

31

Robin turned away again, and nearly lost his balance along with his dignity, but soon steadied both. 'To keep me from finding my way out of this... dream or whatever it is, and back to my friends.'

'Robin.'

Another voice spoke. Calm. Authoritative. It seemed to be in the rocks, the roof, the ground...

Robin smiled, suddenly feeling confident. 'Of course, now that voice I do know. And trust. Herne the Hunter.'

'But you cannot see this "Herne", so why trust him over your own mother. She who stands with you inside this cave.'

'The first fair question of the day.' Robin threw a look back to Maire again, this time keeping his balance expertly. Confidently. 'Experience. That is what tells me I can trust him.'

Lady Maire dropped her hands to her waist, clasped together, the very image of piety and godliness. 'You trust his voice over your own eyes. Eyes that reveal your mother to you?'

'No, you are how I remember my mother.'

'That is what I said,' replied Lady Maire, or whatever she was.

'No, you keep saying you are my mother. Moving past the fact that she is dead, I last saw her when I was, well, barely old enough to tie my own laces. Looking as you do. Which seems hardly likely these many summers later.'

'Is it not better that I come to you now as you recall me from back then?'

'So, you admit you are not truly her? Yes, it is attractive. But not honest.'

'And you prize honesty?'

Robin nodded. 'I have always valued it. I suspect that was something I inherited from my actual mother.'

Lady Maire smiled, still standing in her supplicant, almost virginal, pose. 'Honesty. Trust. Morality. Things we learn from our parents, Robin. But how do we know they are real?'

This stopped Robin in his tracks. 'I don't understand.'

Lady Maire moved her head to one side, ever so slightly. 'You would agree that your concepts, your ideas or morality for instance, are very different from, say, Gisburne's?'

'Of course.'

Lady Maire pressed on. 'But Gisburne would think the same of you. To him, his morality is right and just.'

Robin allowed himself a slight snigger. 'I would be astonished to discover that Gisburne even thinks.'

'Nevertheless, you must acknowledge that you have inherited your parents' view of morality. Of right and wrong.'

Robin conceded this. 'Yes. And furthered by my upbringing by the Miller's family. They were good people too.'

'But what if your morality was skewed, was wrong?'

'Can morality really be wrong, "mother"?' He regarded her carefully. She sounded almost… desperate. As if she was justifying her own actions rather than questioning his. He'd seen this in the Sheriff's soldiers when trying to justify the slaughter of peasants or the destruction of farmlands. Just obeying orders, but yet they knew what they were doing was wrong. 'Surely,' he continued, 'like an opinion, morality is too personal, too shaped by our lives and experiences to be restricted to simple right and wrong?'

Lady Maire tried a different tack. 'What if I told you your father was a bad man?'

'I would not believe you. And it would certainly prove you are not my mother.'

'Do you think of yourself as naive?'

'Do you?'

'Yes,' Lady Maire replied. 'I do.'

Robin thought for a moment, then said: 'Marion has often accused me of being idealistic, but no, not naive.'

Lady Maire let her hands drop, balling her firsts and her eyes flared briefly in anger.

'Then I am sorry to tell you, but your father was responsible for many good things but an equal amount of bad. He was, for want of a better phrase, a monster who massacred many innocents!'

***

Friar Tuck was lost. Well, he reasoned, maybe not lost, but a trifle mislaid. One moment he'd been following John Little through the woods, then something had caught his eye. Once he'd decided it was just the last beat of the sun settling beyond the horizon, John had vanished.

Not literally. People didn't vanish into thin air. They just kept walking, without looking back to check that their diminutive friends were still on their tail.

And unlike John, or Will, or Nasir or, indeed, Robin, Tuck was not terribly good at following tracks. He wasn't really adept at going 'Oh look, that root has recently been trodden upon by a man weighing little more than four bags of corn' or 'dear me, see how that piece of bracken has broken along the stem, suggesting a horse has tiptoed through this copse' or things like that.

Instead he got distracted by thoughts such as 'But, surely, horses do not walk upon tiptoe?' and 'Who really measures the weight of a man by comparing him to bags of corn?'

And precisely because he had become distracted, he had now lost sight of John. And as the darkness came through the woods, he was in danger of losing anything more than about three inches in front of his nose.

Stupid little Friar, he thought. Supposed to be looking for Robin and they'd end up having to send search parties out for him.

Something moved on his peripheral vision.

'John?' he called, perhaps a little too meekly.

He was sure it was a person, but it hadn't been tall enough for John. Or broad enough. But who else could it be?

'Robin?'

But neither Robin nor John replied.

So he must have imagined it.

And now, having glanced in the direction his peripheral vision had dictated, he was no longer on the same path he had been but a few seconds earlier. So, if he walked in a straight line, he'd be further away from John than ever before.

'John?' he called louder. But the only response was a slight wafting of wind through the woods. Maybe that was had caught his eye, a tree branch shifting against the breeze.

This was not a wind to move branches, Tuck. Twigs, perhaps. Leaves. But not branches.

So that had to have been a person he saw.

'Tuck!'

That was John. And it came from… the Friar turned on the spot, listening.

'Yes John?' he yelled back.

'Where are you?'

Ah, no more from that direction.

And Tuck hurried forward, hoping he was on the right path at last.

And hoping that if he had seen someone, he was evading them.

He almost tripped over John as he emerged from the heavily wooden area into a small grassy circular area.

Tuck knew this was one of many this far into the heart of Sherwood Forest. But he wasn't sure he'd ever been into this exact clearing before.

'Have you found him? Found Robin I mean?' Tuck asked, reeved to have found John but stopping himself from giving him a hug of relief to have found his way out of the woods.

'No. Just... this.'

Tuck gasped as he looked down.

John was lifting his left foot from something he had trodden on. Buried a few inches into the ground was a man, barely more than a lad really, his pockmarked face betraying his youth. His eyes were open wide, his face contorted in... fear? Pain? Both?

'Poor soul,' he breathed, and crossed first himself and then the dead body.

John looked up at him. 'Bit late to offer sacraments and crossings, Friar.'

'Who is he? Was he, I mean?'

John shrugged. 'One of the Sheriff's stable boys going by his clothing.'

Little John rose to his full height and looked suspiciously around.

'There's something very odd about this,' he said finally.

'What do you mean?'

John pointed down, without taking his eyes off the trees and woods that hemmed them in. 'I thought at first he had died and been buried. Buried badly. But I'm not so sure now. It's more like...'

Tuck dropped to his knees, patting the man's chest, sharing John's instinct that something was wrong. 'What?' he asked.

'Look at him,' John said, crouching back down alongside Tuck, tracing the edge of the man with his finger. 'It's like he just sunk into the ground. But it's dry as a bone here. And he fits this... grave perfectly. Like it was shaped around him. See how it follows the shape of his arms and legs and... Oh.'

Tuck looked at his companion quizzically.

John carried on. 'His arms. And... yes, his legs. Touch them. Carefully.'

Tuck reached and did so, one at a time. Feeling. Squeezing an—

'Heavens above.'

'I'm not sure heaven had much to do with this,' John muttered.

Tuck pressed down on the left arm. 'It's soft and—'

'Broken,' John finished. 'It's like the ground dragged him down, surrounded him and then squashed him to death.'

'Not possible,' said Tuck. 'And that would be unholy...'

But John was in his element. 'He was alive when it happened. Look at his eyes.'

'I noticed that first of all,' Tuck confirmed. 'Let me close them at least. Poor child. Whoever he was, he did not deserve to die like this.' And the Friar did so.

'I'm not someone who believes in evil, Tuck, but there's something...'

Tuck remembered what he had seen in the woods. That feeling he was being watched, followed. 'Unearthly?'

'That's as good a word as any I suppose.'

Tuck then told John exactly what he had seen and felt in the woods.

'Ordinarily, I'd tell you not to be so daft,' John said. 'But looking at this fellow, I'm not so sure.'

Friar Tuck decided the most he could do right now was what he was trained for. 'Our father who—' he began, but John gripped Tuck's shoulder and eased him upright.

'No time for that. We should move.'

'Why?'

John was again scouring the edges of the clearing, but he pointed at the body. 'Because anything that can do that to a man armed with a sword is not something I care to meet.'

Tuck considered this. He could say a prayer for the poor soldier later. At home. At the camp. If they ever got back.

'Yes, I think I see sense in that.' Then something occurred to. 'John?'

'Friar?'

'What if whatever did that to this poor soul, encountered Robin?'

John looked down at his friend and patted his shoulder in a way that left Tuck utterly less than reassured.

'Then I'd suggest we tread more carefully, so we don't step on him too.'

'You have a dark humour, Little John. Has anyone told you that before?'

But the big man didn't smile back. 'Who said I was joking? Now, come on, let's take that path.'

Tuck decided to stay right on John's tail from now on, treading in his huge footprints if need be.

But he still couldn't shake off the feeling that something was watching them go. And that it had something to do with the poor dead body they had abandoned.

***

Robin was watching his "mother" carefully.

One minute previously, she had stopped talking mid-sentence, as if something – that he couldn't see – had caught her attention. Then she had started twitching her head back and forth, like a cat tracking the mouse it had lost sight of, as it scampered across a floor.

Then she had refocused her attention on him and continued talking as if no such break had happened.

She had been trying to convince him that Lord Ailric, his beloved father was, in truth, a despot and cruel man.

She had yet to offer any proof.

'If I believe you, and I don't,' he said, 'my father – the man you lived with and bore a son – did bad things. Name one.'

The woman, for Robin was convinced by the bile in her tone this was not, nor ever had been, his actual mother, continued as bidden.

'What do you know of the Dragon Lines?'

'The what?'

The not-mother sighed. 'If not for your father, everyone would know of them. Revere them. And of the Dodmen and Dodwomen who divined the lines, who brought these lands together under one enormous power for good.'

Robin actually jumped then, for close in his left ear, he heard the hissed voice of Herne the Hunter.

'Robin? Trust this not.'

In his other, the Dodwoman from Loxley Castle, whose green dress had almost matched her pallor.

'Robin, hear us, reject this vision.'

The not-mother laughed suddenly. 'Oh now I hear them. They are desperate. I can hear your own spirit guides tying to distract you, stop you hearing the truth.'

'You must not be swayed by this vision, Robin,' Herne intoned.

Robin ignored him. For now. 'Fear not, false mother, I know my own mind. Tell me your tale.'

The Lady Maire stood upright, as a priest delivering a sermon might, hands clasped behind her back. She stared straight into Robin's eyes, truly locking him in her sights for the first time.

And Robin actually felt slightly apprehensive at this. She certainly had a powerful gaze.

He certainly couldn't fault the passion in her voice. But he was concerned by the underlying anger that built as she went on. 'The lineage of the Dodmen and Dodwomen goes back many centuries, to when mankind was young and gods walked the earth. The Dodpeople too walked the world, marking out the lines of power that the Dragons would follow. But your father dismissed that power when two of the Dodpeople approached Loxley Castle.'

'Why would he do that?' offered Robin. 'My father was fair. All who knew him have said so.'

His false mother ignored him. She was growing increasingly irate. 'The Dragon Line ran through the castle, my son. The castle broke the line, disturbed the ancient powers, so the Dodpeople requested it be taken down, rebuilt elsewhere. A reasonable request. Your father had the Dodman killed to silence him. His unfortunate wife fled in fear for her life. Justifiably, I believe. The poor, poor woman, scared for her life...'

'And Father did all this with no fair hearing? No counsel from his peers?' Robin slowly shook his head. 'That sounds... unlikely.'

The mockery of Maire finally lost her temper. Robin stood his ground, watching as her face twisted in fury, her eyes staring wildly, her features momentarily changing into a heavily lined and twisted version of his beautiful mother. 'You didn't know your father! Who are you to determine his character?

'I am Robin of Loxley. And I know myself. And I know that the blood of my mother and father, which runs through me, would never be so cold and dismissive.' He locked eyes with her, and her face lost some of its lunatic fire. 'Now, who are you? Really?'

Robin felt a presence solidify beside him. Still shadowed, still not quite there in reality, more like an apparition than anything else. But he knew who it was. He had felt that presence before.

'She is a phantom,' Herne stated plainly and clearly

Robin dropped to one knee at the sound of his voice, the confirmation of his presence. 'Herne! My lord...'

The Woman in Green was there too, at his other side, similarly just a shadow. The Dodwoman she called herself. The word the false Maire had used in her story. Her lies about his father.

'Oh he's very subservient, isn't he Herne?' she laughed. 'Do get up, Robin. You'll catch a chill kneeling in that damp.'

'You are not helping, Ancient One,' Herne boomed.

Robin was back on his feet, taking in the beings either side of him, both now fully formed

'Why are you here now? I heard you in my head, but you are actually with me in this... whatever this is.'

The Dodwoman waved a hand casually around the cavern. 'Like the castle beforehand, it's a dreamscape. Created by the spirit of the past and present, of might-have-beens, and never-coulds.' She then pointed at the Lady Maire. 'Created by her.'

The phantom sneered directly at the green-clad Dodwoman. 'Why are you here? At his side? You should be castigating this son of Ailric!'

But Herne was having none of it. He stepped forward, placing himself between her and Robin and the Dodwoman.

'Hear the words of Herne, phantom spirit. As Keeper of the Oaks, Patriarch of the Wild Hunt and Spirit of the Natural World, Herne the Hunter casts you back out into the world. Desist from this phantasm of reality.'

Nothing happened. Then the Lady Maire roared with laughter.

'You think you have power over me, Hunter? Over my world? My mystic arcana was ancient before you were even cursed into existence. You present no threat to me.'

'Herne is all-powerful, "Maire". You really don't want to make an enemy of him.'

Their foe just laughed again.

So Robin stepped forward, indeed in front of Herne. 'Fake mother, this time it is I who demand you leave.'

'You? Oh, who are you to make demands, child of evil?'

And Robin crossed back to her until he was standing almost nose to nose. 'Me? I am Robin I'the Hood, the Hooded Man, sworn to protect these lands – and you are a threat. A threat to be taken down. Now.'

And for Robin, everything went black.

CHAPTER FIVE

Suddenly Robin was back outside. The open air, sweet night air, the winter moon above illuminating the tips of tall trees and the crisp wet grass.

'Well, that went well,' said the Dodwoman, and Robin stared, amazed, as once again her clothing changed, the green dress reforming as her original hooded cloak, which she tugged around herself for warmth.

Robin looked around. 'We are near Loxley Castle. We should get into Sherwood Forest before the Sheriff's night sentries find us.' He stopped suddenly and put his hand to his head. 'And I have an ache in my head stronger than anything mead could have created.'

The Dodwoman ignored his complaining and instead walked in a circle around him. 'Why *here* I wonder?'

Robin looked at her. 'What do you mean by that?'

'She took you while you slept in your camp. Why return you here and not there?'

'Does it matter?'

The Dodwoman nodded. 'She never does anything without a reason. This place must have significance. To her. Something she wants you to be aware of.'

Robin shrugged. 'It's one of the least safe places in the sight of the castle. This leads to the main path, that way takes us directly into Sherwood.'

The Dodwoman stood where Robin indicated and stared up at the castle. 'Of course.'

'And?' Robin said after a few seconds, hoping for an explanation.

The Dodwoman sighed. 'So if she were telling the truth – and whilst it's debateable, to her it was real – then after Thane Ailric, Lord of Loxley killed her husband and she fled, this would have been her last view of the castle, and, in essence, of her husband. A focus for the forthcoming years of rage and anguish. And all brought forth here, before she entered Sherwood Forest.'

'Are you saying she never came out again?'

The Dodwoman shrugged. 'Possibly. Could anyone live in there for decades?'

Robin laughed. 'We survive in there and know the forest well enough to evade capture, but I doubt we could stay there without leaving for food and so forth. The only person who…'

Robin trailed off.

'Go on,' urged the Dodwoman.

Robin thought hard. 'When I was a boy, there was an old woman who lived in a cottage at the heart of the forest. No one from any of the villages or castles paid her any heed. She was rumoured to be a witch.'

'Of course she was. What else would you imagine of a lone woman? Typical peasants.'

'We used to dare each other to go to the cottage, to try and glimpse her and her cauldron. When I was about ten, I went. Me, Much, Adam, Ben… we went to find her. The Scavenger we called her then. And she caught us. Adam and Much bolted but Ben and I, we just stood there. And she looked at us, at me. I was terrified, it seemed as though she looked through me, and I felt cold. So cold. And then suddenly she just yelled at us like a madwoman and we turned and ran.'

'What happened to her?'

Robin shrugged. 'Ben and I reckoned she must've died. She had to be over a hundred by then.'

The Dodwoman smiled. 'You'll be surprised how long hate can sustain you, especially when you are already imbued with certain… powers from the land.'

But Robin wasn't listening. He remembered the vision. The Great Hall, after the imaginary poisoning.

'Ben Hockleaf. Son of Clem, my father's man at arms.'

The Dodwoman frowned, she wasn't following, for once.

'I haven't seen Ben in years. He works for the Sheriff these days, along with Peter, Richard all our old friends. They had no option. So why was he the one in that vision or whatever you called it, warning us about dragons?'

The Dodwoman nodded slowly. 'I suspect your friend Ben may have met her recently. She probably didn't let him go this time.'

'You mean the old witch, the Scavenger, is that woman pretending to be my mother in our visions?'

The Dodwoman nodded. 'I imagine so. We can be very vindictive.'

Robin's eyes widened. 'She is a Dodwoman, then. That story she told had some grain of truth. But you're a Dodwoman too.'

'I am the original. The first lady of the Dod People to walk this earth with my husband, mapping the Dragon Lines.'

'Then you must be very aged. And you don't appear that way to me. And Herne knew you, are you as old as him?'

'Oh, I'm far older than Herne the Hunter, Robin. And in my time, far more powerful. My people controlled and soothed the great beasts – sent them to rest beneath the ground, sung the Lines to enchant them. Imprison them if you like, so mankind could thrive. That was our task.'

'Then what happened?'

The Dodwoman sighed and began walking towards the forest. 'You said it wasn't safe to stay out here. You may be right, for any number of reasons. And we should find Herne, work out where she placed him.'

'He wasn't with us just now. Why not?'

'Herne is part of Sherwood Forest, you know that. He can't survive out here, so he'll be back in there. Somewhere. I hope.' She smiled. 'He's a tedious chap and terribly dull, but the world can't survive without him, so we must ensure his welfare.'

Then they crossed the threshold into Sherwood Forest and left the so-called civilised world behind.

As they pushed through the undergrowth, the Dodwoman continued her tales.

'For hundreds of generations our offspring, in loving pairs, maintained the paths, the lines, keeping the power strong and intact. Then, twenty years ago, a Dodman approached your father, to alert him to the fact that Loxley Castle had been constructed on one of these ancient lines of power. Its foundations had broken the line.'

Robin gasped. 'Are you saying that… phantom was speaking the truth?'

'Of the encounter? Absolutely. Of the result – I cannot be sure. Either way, my descendant died. Whether by Ailric's hand, some other or simply an accident, even I cannot know.'

'And the phantom pretending to be my poor mother?'

'Well, she's no true phantom. Indeed, she is as real as you, living here in Sherwood Forest, using her arcana to deceive and entrap you as she has so many descendants of your father's friends and workers. There has been a spate of deaths in the last few months and Herne realised they were not entirely natural. Soon, he began to see the link between them all.'

'So he contacted you? How?'

The Dodwoman chuckled. 'Oh, we have our ways, but they are not your concern. One of the most recent was a young man working at Nottingham castle, a Welsh lad by the name of Samuel Tully. She made the earth itself take him. Herne attempted to persuade the ground to give up its new treasure, but it wouldn't listen. He still lies somewhere within Sherwood Forest, half buried, half-exposed, a warning to Herne and me of how powerful she is. I should imagine your friend Benjamin Hockleaf has met a similar fate and she used his image to talk to you, to play with you. I doubt his death at her hands was an accident. She'll have remembered him from your childhood and waited. She's very good at waiting.'

Robin sighed. 'Poor Ben. He tried to warn me...'

'Robin!'

Robin and the Dodwoman turned to find themselves facing Herne the Hunter.

He looked... drained, exhausted. Robin had never seen him like this before. Where he stood in the moonlight, the plants closest to him were withing, curling up as they watched.

'She is... strong,' he said. 'And I fear I cannot help you further today. When the Dodwoman and I realised how powerful our enemy was, I tried to get you out of the dreamscape into which she had cast you into by taking you to your true friends in the Forest, but I wasn't able to stop her throwing you further out.'

'Will you be all right?' asked Robin, aware that there was little he would be able to do in any case.

Herne shook his head. 'I need time and I fear while I am weakened, I cannot help you.'

'I am so sorry. I should return to Marion and the others and get some rest before we fight anew. My head is raging as if I had been kicked upside by a mule and—'

But Herne held up hand. 'Robin, wait. We didn't only rescue you. This is not over yet. Somewhere in Sherwood Forest is a point where all the local Dragon Lines converge, a seat of tremendous unearthly power.'

Seeing Herne's distress, his difficulty in finding the energy to talk, the foliage around him decaying further with every heartbeat, caused Robin to fall into a pained silence. The Dodwoman continued on his behalf.

'So yes, we believe your phantom mother is the wife of that Dodman who died in Loxley Castle. The latest Dodwoman of my lineage. And she seeks revenge. I fear Sam Tully and Benjamin Hockleaf will not be the last deaths on my conscience if she is not stopped.'

'But how can I find her?' wondered Robin. 'Especially while my head is killing me.'

'A residual pain from your meeting of minds. Remember that headache, Robin. It may come in useful,' said Herne.

And then he was gone.

The Dodwoman sighed. 'It's just you and me now.' She reached out and took Robin's shoulders. 'You have to find the Point of Power and lure her into it.'

'In my dream, Ben mentioned that. So how exactly do I find it?

'Herne would probably say something portentous like "Oh Robin, you must feel the power which runs through the Forest."'

'And should I?'

'If we had ten years for you to learn the art of divining and reading the Dragon lines, certainly. But time is short and I have a better plan.'

Robin took a step back involuntarily. 'Better than that of Herne himself?'

'Oh Robin, you have to stop giving him so many airs and graces. He's a great man... well, a great spirit and incredibly powerful and yes, you owe much to him. But he's also terribly single-minded and unimaginative. No, you need the wiles of a Dodwoman. To fight fire with fire.'

'I do not like where this is going...'

The Dodwoman smiled and clapped her hands. 'Good, you shouldn't. Now, tell me, do you know what a Judas Goat is?'

***

Friar Tuck and John Little were starting to think about giving up the hunt for Robin.

It was dark, getting colder, and if he were conscious, they'd have found him by now. If he were lying unconscious somewhere, the chances of finding him in the darkness, this far into Sherwood Forest's heart, was negligible.

'Marion will crucify us,' John muttered, 'if we go back empty handed.'

Tuck caressed the crucifix hung around his neck as John said that but, sadly, he agreed with the sentiment.

He decided to change the subject.

'I wonder who that lad was. He was little older than Robin.'

John clicked his tongue in annoyance. 'Tuck, he worked for the Sheriff. I'm not wasting my time mourning him.'

'It was a particularly horrible way to die.'

John shrugged. 'Are there any good ways? Besides, I am quite certain the Church has occasioned worse.'

Tuck didn't speak for a moment as they walked on but thought about what John had said. There seemed so much bitterness in his tone.

'Do you dislike and distrust me as much as you do the Church, John?'

John stopped, his shoulders slumping slightly, as if he'd expecting this discussion but didn't want it.

'Look, you are one man, Tuck and I have seen where your loyalties and your heart lie. That makes you a friend. But I would not recommend you never test my contempt for your church.'

Tuck reached out and took John's arm.

'Very well. But remember this – for every corrupt representative of God that you meet, there are dozens of good ones who stand against evil. Just as you do. As do we all.'

'If you say so,' was John's only response as he eased away from Tuck's touch and moved forward.

But Tuck stood still. This had to be said.

'I may have renounced the physical church and chapel where I worked, but I will never abandon God. For every soul who corrupts his Word for evil purposes, there are ten who believe in its goodness. And we are far more devout.'

John sighed and looked down at his companion.

'What's brought this on?'

Tuck shrugged. The cold was getting to him even through his thick robes. He wasn't thinking just about Robin's fate now, but of his own mortality, not just here and now, but in the hereafter, where he would answer for the choices made in Sherwood.

'Because whatever killed that lad, it was a power that should not be allowed to flourish on this good Earth. And just as you would use your strength and Robin his bow, and Will his guile, I shall… I must use my faith to help stop it.'

John almost smiled. 'You're an odd one, Friar.'

Tuck smiled back. 'And that has been said more than once before. But the fact is, our merrie band has been drawn together under unusual circumstances. That makes strange bedfellows of us all, but if we are to survive what is coming, it is our trust in one another that shall surely be our salvation.'

***

The Dodwoman pulled her green hood around her head, as she watched Robin walk away from her and through the bushes.

Then she lowered her gaze to the ground and smiled. After a moment, a familiar voice echoed inside her head.

But there was no physical manifestation to match it. Not this time. Just his ethereal presence.

'What now, Dodwoman?' Herne's voice asked her.

She replied without shifting her gaze from the floor of the forest. 'Robin has gone, ready to start his mission. We can only wait. We may not help any more than we have. Besides, my time here in his reality is almost over.'

Herne's voice seemed to get softer, almost concerned perhaps. 'You realise that if he stops your descendant, this Scavenger woman, and she dies, there are no Dodpeople left, no one to wander the world, protecting the lines? The Beasts would awaken and roam the world once more.'

The Dodwoman laughed gently. 'Oh don't worry, mighty Hunter. There are thousands of Dodpeople still. The Scavenger is but one renegade. The difference is, she has used these past years to turn her innate arcana to darkness.'

'So, stopping her won't destroy the world?'

'Not at all,' she relied. 'Failing to stop her however, almost certainly will.' She finally raised her eyes and stared at the area which Robin had strode away through. 'You have, in him, a fine Champion.' She paused, not wanting to ask the next question, but knowing she had to. 'What will you do when he's gone?'

'Why should he go anywhere?' asked Herne.

'Oh Herne, you know as I do, as all the Spirit Walkers do, that Robin of Loxley has, at most, two years left.' And she felt a chill go through her, not her body but through her mind as erne reacted. 'Oh,' she said sadly. 'Oh, you haven't told him, have you?'

'This is not a topic for you and me to discuss, Ancient One.'

The Dodwoman accepted the admonishment. 'Of course. But know this, I will grieve alongside you, when it is his time.'

***

Little John and Friar Tuck were retracing their steps, back to the encampment, their search for Robin having proven fruitless. Both were feeling the cold and damp of the night air and had only the moon to guide them.

Tuck had wondered about starting a fire, creating torches, but John had been concerned that on a night like this, both flame and smoke might draw the night sentries from Nottingham Castle.

Tuck agreed with his reasoning, as he blew into his numbing hands to keep them warm.

It wasn't working. 'I'm sure this isn't the correct path back,' he said.

'It is,' John said with the finality of someone who would brook no further argument.

'Perhaps Robin doesn't want to be found.'

John frowned down at him. 'What do you mean by that?'

'Well, now that Marion has joined us, he has what he thought he's always wanted. But perhaps, just perhaps, he's having second thoughts. Many men do shortly before they get married.'

John stopped walking. 'Are Robin and Marion getting married?'

Tuck blew into his palms again. 'Well, no, not that they've said, but surely you can see it'll happen eventually.'

'Maybe. But even if that was the case, I don't see Robin hiding. He's not the type to do that.'

Tuck decided to change the subject again. 'Are you sure you can get us back in the dark? I still think we came from…'

'I have already told you, I know the way. Just make sure you don't get left behind. Again.'

Tuck nodded. 'Of course. I'll be following in your footsteps. Literally.'

'Religiously.'

'Very funny,' Tuck grunted. 'Though I still think we came from the east—'

They were nearly knocked off their feet as Robin bowled through the bushes ahead of them.

Their attempts at greeting were cut short as he held up a hand. Both men immediately knew better than to argue.

'Have you seen anything unusual. Anyone odd?'

Tuck smiled. 'John's *quite* odd. '

John cut him off. 'What do you mean?'

Robin sighed. 'I… I'm not sure. Anything unusual.'

'Well, in this forest, anything's possible.'

Tuck shook John's sleeve. 'The body.'

'What body?'

'We found a body,' Tuck repeated, rather pointlessly.

'Yes, I guessed that,' said Robin. 'What was strange about it?'

John took up the story. 'The way he died. His entire body had been crushed. And not be a tree but by the earth itself.'

Robin nodded. 'Sounds likely. Show me, please.'

John strode forward. 'This way.'

Tuck pointed east. 'I think it was more that way.'

But Robin and John were already hurrying away in the opposite direction.

'Well, that's just rude,' Tuck muttered. Then remembered what happened last time he let John roam out of view. He decided, too, that he ought to tell Robin about his feeling that they were being followed. With a last grunt of 'I still think it was that way…'

Tuck followed his friends.

***

Not far from where Robin, Tuck and John had just moved away from, was a dense copse, the branches of the trees cutting out all moonlight from above, creating a thick dark circle. At the centre of the darkness was a small hut. An old shack made from hundreds of twigs and branches, woven together by old cloth.

Unlike when Benjamin Hockleaf and Sam Tully had found it, it was lit from inside by a roaring fire. The flames were keeping the night chills away from the Scavenger woman, her frayed black cloak in danger of immolating at any second as a twig or piece of bark crackled and spat a tiny fire spark in its direction.

It was full of many such burn holes, but none had caused real damage. The Scavenger was too quick, too observant for that. She may indeed have been over a hundred years old, judging by her face, stretched as it was against her skull, which itself showed through the thin skin reflecting the firelight. Bony arms and skeletal fingers caressed a wooden branch second before it was tossed into the pyre.

But her eyes were as bright and alive as they had been all those years before when she and her husband had arrived in Sherwood, and her life had changed forever.

Before the madness consumed her.

'He's getting closer. With every heartbeat, he gets closer to his last – and the line of Loxley will be extinguished forever.' She turned her head to stare at her companion. 'Then, of course, there's the rest of them to mop up. But Loxley is the pinnacle, don't you think Benjamin?'

There was no reply.

'Nothing to say on the subject? Well, I respect that. Sorry you had to see what happened to your friend Sam, but I never could stand the Welsh. They never understood the dragons and other great beasts.'

She pointed to the fire.

'Fancy a bit of leg, Benny, my boy? Or a chunk of fatted shoulder? No? Not hungry? Oh well, don't blame you. Hope you don't mind if I do, though. Need to get my strength up for the fight that's coming.' She cackled to herself. 'And what a fight it is going to be…'

And with another laugh she reached over to Benjamin Hockleaf's dead, decaying body and tugged a chunk of his shoulder away from his body, biting into it, licking her lips in delight as she did so.

CHAPTER SIX

R obin was kneeling next to the body of Sam Tully, the tiny corpse barely lit by the moonlight, which had moved to the far side of Sherwood Forest.

At John's suggestion, he touched the legs and arms, feeling the pulverised bones. He stood, blowing air out of his cheeks.

'She's truly using her dark arcana powers.'

'Who is?' asked John.

'I don't know her name. Or what she truly looks like. But I know where she lives.'

'That helps,' said Tuck.

'This is Sam Tully. He was a friend of a… friend. And just for that, for being in the wrong place at the wrong time…' Robin indicated his body.

Friar Tuck nodded. 'And is this someone after you too?'

Robin nodded sadly.

'Is this anything to do with the Sheriff? Or Gisburne?' asked John.

'No,' said Robin. 'This is far darker than anything either of them are capable of. Right now, I need to go to her. Take the battle straight there.'

He told them all that had happened, brushing aside their incredulity about visions, his mother's image and green-clad Dodwomen. He didn't mention Herne's involvement – some things needed to remain private.

Nonetheless, he told them about the Scavenger woman from his childhood, and about Ben and Sam. And about the cottage at the heart of Sherwood Forest.

And John and Tuck listened, not interrupting, knowing that this was not the time to put pressure on Robin, but to listen. And support.

'What do you need us to do?' asked Tuck when Robin had finished his astonishing tale.

'Get back to camp, get the others out of Sherwood Forest until I have put an end to this.'

'Will's there. And Nasir. They can look after Marion and Much,' said John.

Tuck tried to soften the atmosphere. 'Actually, it's probably the other way round. Marion's very adept with a sword these days.'

Robin's demeanour suggested that he was in no mood for Tuck's wit. 'I'd still feel happier if you were there too.'

John snorted. 'So what… we leave you to face someone, something, that can do… this? Alone?'

Tuck nodded at John. 'Oh, you should know us better than that Robin.'

Robin realised there was no point in arguing. 'And you are right about Will and Nasir. And Marion, frankly. So, thank you my friends. But it might be dangerous.'

'Good. I'm bored of walking through the forest, trying not to punch Friar Tuck.'

'Hey!' Tuck protested. Then nudged Robin. 'Mind you, he's not wrong. I can be a very annoying companion.'

'So, punching someone else would be better for him *and* me,' John said.

Robin agreed. 'Let's go. It's getting darker and colder and I would rather not face this woman at midnight.' He started to lead them back the way they had come, but then stopped. 'Oh, and John?'

'Robin?'

'Please don't punch Tuck. Well, not too hard…'

John nodded and Tuck waggled a finger at them, as if telling off two naughty schoolboys.

But all three of them knew, without needing to tell the others, that this was a fight from which they may not return.

***

The Scavenger, sat in her hut, lit by the flickering orange flames, smiled to herself. And threw a quick smile to Benjamin Hockleaf's rapidly diminishing corpse.

'Got to get my strength up, Benny my boy. I don't think Robin's going to exactly be a pushover.' She tore a chunk of hot flesh from the shoulder she had been holding in the fire. She then reached over to the body with it. 'Tasty. Want a bit? No? No, you're right, probably not appropriate in the circumstances.'

Then she stopped. That had been the sound of a carefully positioned set of brittle twigs being snapped by a careless boot.

'Hear that?' she whispered. 'I think we've been rumbled…'

More than rumbled, she realised, as the door to her shack disintegrated into a shower of twigs and rags, Robin kicking his way through it.

'I believe you've been expecting me?'

'Indeed, I have, Robin of Loxley.' She remained seated, staring into the fire, a smile on her lips. 'I shall place your body in the Point of Power to appease my ancestors.'

'Which is… where?'

The Scavenger laughed and shook her head. 'A fine attempt, Loxley.' She reached beneath her. 'Here,' she said suddenly. 'Catch'

With a gasp, Robin looked down, to find a dagger embedded in his breast.

'Sorry, did that hurt?' she asked him.

Robin had dropped to one knee, flailing, trying to draw the dagger out.

'This… cannot hurt me…' But the blood bubbling through his mouth and trickling down his chin suggested he was wrong. But just to make sure, the Scavenger jumped up, with the ease of someone sixty years her junior, reached over and viciously twisted the hilt left, then right, then left again.

'Time to die, Loxley. Die. In pain.'

And he did. She watched as the life left his eyes forever, and his body slumped forward, easing the dagger deeper into his no longer pumping heart.

After a few seconds, she lifted his head, stared into his blood-soaked face. 'My family has had their vengeance at last.' She released her grip, allowing him to slump once more, crossed back to her seat and flopped down. She glanced over to Ben's corpse.

'You're off the hook, Benny. My larder has been replenished.'

***

Robin, John and Tuck were approaching the dark copse where Robin knew the shack to be.

And then he coughed, and gasped, dropping to one knee.

John was at his side in an instant.

'Robin? What's the matter?'

Robin tried to wave aside his ministrations aside, but he failed because the pain he was in was too great, and in the end, he gratefully accepted John's help in getting him back to his feet.

'Another… vision. A dream. We must be close, she's putting 'mares into my head.'

Tuck frowned. 'How bad?'

Robin managed a little chuckle. 'Oh she just successfully killed me.'

Tuck and John exchanged a look of concern. Then Tuck pushed a smile onto his face as he addressed Robin.

'Did I get the chance to give you the sacraments?'

Robin shook his head. 'Ha. No… wait a moment – Tuck, you may have just saved us. Saved me.'

Tick grinned widely. 'Really? Oh good. Umm, how?'

'Because you were not in the vision – and I suspect that means she doesn't realise you two are here.'

'Which helps how?' asked John.

Robin tapped his nose conspiratorially. 'Surprise. Distraction. Might be the edge we need. To find this Point of Power she mentioned.' He winced suddenly. 'And the pounding headache I've got suggests we may have found our enemy.'

He parted some bushes and sure enough, at the centre of the tiny clearing amongst the thick trees was the shack, exactly as he remembered it from his childhood.

He looked at his loyal companions. 'Time for both of you to do as we discussed. Go now.'

John frowned. 'And just what are you going to do?'

'Exactly what I was told to do. Play the Judas Goat.'

***

The Scavenger sat in her hut, lit by the flickering orange flames, and smiled to herself. And threw a quick smile to Benjamin Hockleaf's rapidly diminishing corpse.

'Got to get my strength up, Benny, my boy. I don't think Robin's going to exactly be a pushover.' She tore a chunk of hot flesh from the shoulder she had been holding in the fire. She then reached over to the body with it. 'Tasty. Want a bit? No? No, you're right, probably not appropriate in the circumstances.'

Then she stopped. That had been the sound of a carefully positioned set of brittle twigs being snapped by a careless boot.

'Hear that?' she whispered. 'I think we've been rumbled…'

More than rumbled, she realised, as the door to her shack disintegrated into a shower of twigs and rags, Robin kicking his way through it.

'I believe you've been expecting me?'

'Indeed, I have, Robin of Loxley.' She remained seated, staring into the fire, a smile on her lips.

'Who is your friend there?'

The Scavenger glanced aside. 'Who him? Benjamin Something-or-other. I think you used to play in these woods together. He's not a particularly sparkling conversationalist, I have to say.' She held a hand up, to stop Robin saying anything else. ''Scuse me. Got something stuck in my teeth. Must be something I ate.' And she threw another glance at Ben's body; Robin saw the vast quantities of missing flesh.

The Scavenger had to admire his ability not to retch.

Instead, he fixed his gaze back upon her. 'I gather you want me dead.'

'That's the plan.' She chuckled, then spat some of Ben's gristle into the flames where it bubbled and spat. 'You are so like him.'

'Who? Benjamin there?'

'No. No, your father.' The Scavenger finally looked Robin squarely in the face. 'The sanctimonious Thane Ailric.'

'I don't really remember him.'

The Scavenger rose up. Standing before Robin, she dropped her hands to her waist, clasped together, the very image of piety and godliness – mirroring the pose she had taken while wearing the Lady Maire's form. 'Yes, so very like you. Charming. Disarming. Equally good-looking. And devious as they come.' She leaned forward, gave a long, hard sniff, and nodded, as if working something out.

'Still got the scents of the spirits on you. Been talking to my ancestor again, have you?'

Robin pictured the Woman in Green, the original Dodwoman. 'I can see a lot of her in your face, too.'

'Family lines run deep in the Dodpeople,' she said. 'But the morality, and choosing of sides, that's not always inherited or bestowed.' She sniffed again. 'Ooh and I can smell that old fraud Herne himself, if I'm not mistaken. I thought I'd got rid of him in the cavern.'

'Why did you abuse my memory of my mother? Why not just appear as you?'

'Where's the fun in that? And, more importantly, it was a good way to make you listen.'

Robin nodded. 'Fair point. So, you believe my father did you a great wrong.'

The Scavenger nodded and began pacing the tiny area of the shack, running her thick fingers along the twigs, bracken and rags at random intervals. 'I was there, with my beloved. I don't believe, I know.'

'And this mistake, if such an error even happened,' said Robin, 'justifies you murdering everyone associated with Loxley Castle?'

Without hesitation, the Scavenger nodded. And smiled.

Robin's hand went to the sword at his hip. 'You're mad.'

And with sudden volume and savagery, she let out a screech and pointed at Robin's heart. 'Then you really ought to humour me. You saw in your mind how fast I am with a dagger.'

Robin kept his hand on the hilt of his sword. 'You haven't used it though.'

'That was the dress rehearsal. No, I'm going to savour this moment. Benny there was my first attempt. His fate will be yours.'

'Skinned alive? Stock for your larder?'

'After a fashion. Sorry, hold on, still a bit of muscle in my teeth.' She used her other hand to scratch around in her mouth, then flicked something onto the ground. 'There we go. Now, where was I? Oh yes…'

And she suddenly threw both arms straight upwards, towards the feeble roof of her shack.

The ground shook in time with a massive crash of thunder. Not only was it the loudest Robin had ever heard, but it seemed to be focused on the local area. No, on this copse itself.

On this shack.

'Sounds like bad weather coming,' he said as lightly as he could over the noise.

'This ends. Now.' The Scavenger stretched her fingers out even further, and Robin could only stand aghast as the shack disintegrated into a maelstrom of twigs and branches, leaves and rags, freed from their long entwinement and now acting like a thousand tiny daggers swirling round the two of them at colossal speed.

With an exultant cry, the Scavenger kept one arm pointed straight up and lowered the other to point at Robin's pounding heart.

'I have waited years for this moment. Time to die, Robin. Time. To. Die!'

***

John and Tuck were in the dark, on all fours, feeling the ground. There was no longer any moonlight to aid them, they had nothing but their own night vision and the sense of touch.

'Where is it, where is it?' Tuck moaned. 'It was around here earlier…' Then there was soft, squelching sound and Tuck groaned loudly.

'Ewww, I've found it.'

John pulled the Friar back. 'Tuck! You're kneeling on the poor boy. Help me get him out of this hole.'

'John, it's hard to get a grip, everything under his skin is just… liquid.'

But John didn't give up. He threw clods of earth aside as he tried to work the saggy body of Sam Tully free from its unearthly entombment.

'If Robin is right, if this is this so-called Point of Power, we must get Sam's body out of it. Or he won't be able to do what needs got be done.'

'I know! I'm trying.'

'You should be used to dead bodies in your line of work.'

Tuck was growing tired at the jokes at his expense but was determined not to show it. 'Yes, and they often smell a bit, but they tend not to ooze under my grip.'

And with a final grunt from each of them, they launched Sam's body out of the ground. John struggled to maintain a hold on it.

'It's like trying to hold a bolster filled with water,' he said, carefully balancing the corpse, trying not to let it slop to the ground again. 'What now?'

Tuck crossed himself again. 'We should probably give him a decent burial.'

John snorted. 'We just yanked him out of one hole in the ground. I'm not digging another to put him back in.

But Tuck was adamant. 'Until Robin needs us, we have nothing else to do. And it's the right thing to do too. You know that, John Little.'

If Tuck was using his full name, John knew it was time to be serious. He began to scour the trees in search of dead branches strong enough to serve Tuck as a spade.

***

Robin was struggling to stay upright, such was the force of the winds whipping around him and the Scavenger.

He took his hand from his sword and yelled above the awful sound.

'I surrender.'

'What?'

'I said I— oh, never mind.' He yelled louder. 'I don't know what my father did to your husband or why, but if it will stop you killing anyone else, I surrender to you.'

But the Scavenger was having none of it. 'Really? That kind of thing may fool that numbskull who calls himself a Sheriff, but I'm not that daft.'

Quiet enough that she could not hear, Robin muttered 'Of that, I am not so sure…'

He turned his back on her and prepared to walk into the screeching winds whipping around.

'Where are you going?'

'Home.'

The Scavenger laughed. 'Try walking through this maelstrom, you'll be cut to pieces.'

'If you're going to kill me anyway, what difference will it make?' And he threw the most contemptuous look back at her that he could manage under the circumstances. 'Besides, I'm not convinced you can really do it.'

'What do you mean?' the Scavenger wailed over the storm.

The remains of Benjamin Hockleaf were suddenly scooped up too and dissipated in the wind, adding chunks of rotted flesh and bone to the daggers of wood. He yelled back at her. 'You just blew your home apart with a thunderbolt, and if you really wanted me dead, that would have been the time. And no daggers either. You can't actually do it outside a dream. And, for all I know, this is just another of your pathetic visions.'

There was another ground-shaking crash of thunder and through the haze of flotsam, Robin thought he saw the earth beneath the copse break apart a fraction.

'I think you'll find there's little I can't do, Robin of Loxley.'

And Robin let his anger flare up suddenly.

'Except tell me what you think my father did.'

And like a candle being blown out, the wind and noise stopped and all that remained of the shack lay scattered across the ground of the copse. Robin noted that he had been correct, a small chasm had opened, a few steps away.

And although it was against every fibre of his being, Robin turned tail and ran.

Ran for his life.

***

She shrieked in fury at Robin's departing form.

'You want a chase, boy?' she snarled to herself. 'So be it.'

And she headed off after him, ignoring any tree branches, twigs, weeds, everything between her and her prey.

She could see some paces ahead, Robin slashing at branches with his sword.

The fool, she thought, that'll use up your precious energy.

She needed no such aids. The power of her twisted, insane mind, utilising the dark arcana she had practised over many years, meant that with the slightest click of her fingers, any obstacles withered and turned to dust in less than the time it took for her to wish it so.

Finally, however, she lost sight of him through one last thicket of shrubs and trees. No matter. With one easy click of a finger, those plants likewise simply burst into dust and nothingness.

And there he was, sword in hand, exhausted and fighting for breath but facing her.

So, she stopped running and let herself walk the last few yards towards him.

She hadn't felt this powerful, this young in years. Everything she had been planning for, dreaming of, plotting and scheming over, it was all coming together, leading to this exact moment.

Midnight.

At the Point of Power.

Did he realise that was where he stood? Maybe. Maybe not. Such knowledge would not help him now.

Revenge was hers at last.

'Well? You chased after me, so you must have something to say now?' Robin yelled at her.

She stopped a foot in front of him, just out of reach of his sword.

But, just in case, she clicked her fingers and the sword flew out of his hand to land… somewhere far and distant.

'This, Robin, this is the Point of Power. The Nexus where the ley lines, the ancient paths of Dragon power, that we Dodpeople have guarded for centuries, lies. And here is where you die.'

Why wasn't he scared? Begging for his life?

'So you keep saying. But I have no interest in that. I thought you might be able to tell me something about my father, but it seems that you know nothing.'

All right, you asked for it, she thought. 'You want to know about your father? He was a liar, a charlatan. A man of deceit and treachery. He invited us to feast with him. With your mother. The noblemen of his court, as well as his soldiers and servants.'

'My father never stood on ceremony.'

She could picture so clearly in her mind. Even after all these years, the image was so fresh. So poignant. The beginning of the end.

'We feasted upon meats and fruits from many lands. And my husband, my beloved, he ate poisoned fruit. His face went red, his neck swelled up and he could not breathe. He was dead in seconds.'

And again, Robin was bleating on about his wretched father. 'I'm sorry, but how is that my father's fault?'

Everything she had spent decades saying in her mind, the words she would use, the emotions on which she would prey to destroy Thane Ailric's useless offspring – now was her moment.

'Your father poisoned him. Scared of the powers that we represented. Of the ancient ley lines we told him of. He. Murdered. My. Husband!'

Robin was scared, she could see that now. He was cracking under the pressure, she was sure. Soon he would cry, he would beg her to end his worthless life, he would – why wouldn't he stop talking?

'His face grew scarlet, you said? He couldn't breathe?'

'His neck was swollen, ready to burst!' she screamed. 'I can still see it now. I see it every day!'

And still Robin stood tall, not on his knees as she had pictured this moment. Still he jabbered.

'I have heard tales from overseas,' he was saying, 'both from the Sheriff's court and my friend Nasir. Of people who eat certain foods, or are stung by bees and wasps. They die not of not poison but of a natural reaction to something their own body cannot tolerate.'

He paused meaningfully.

"Nature can be dangerous, I'm sure you'll agree."

She would not listen any longer. This was her moment. Her revenge. For all the injustices. 'Poison! He was murdered!'

How dare he? In the midst of her vengeance, speak of accidents. Deny his father's responsibility.

She would show him.

The Scavenger threw her arms skywards again and let out a primal scream of pain and rage.

The firmament itself responded with a sound louder than either had ever heard, as a huge crack split the ground asunder.

She stared at Robin and then at the cracks. Surely, he was losing his balance as the ground shook in pain from the torture that she was inflicting upon it.

Was that Herne she could hear in her head? Howling in agony as his precious Sherwood was ripped into two, three, four, five...

'Look, Robin,' she screeched at the useless boy. 'There. See the cracks in the land. That was where Sam Tully was lying – the Point of Power. The assembly point for all the Dragon Paths of the land. I can feel the power of the earth flowing into me – and you are going down there.'

Robin was finally on his knees, trying not to topple into the chasms surrounded him.

'You will shatter the forest – that crack is getting larger by the second. All of Nottingham could fall!'

Nottingham? Ha! The stupid child, did he not realise how far her rage would spread. The whole of the isles of Britain would be destroyed. The Dodpeople's revenge.

'Then fall it will,' she bellowed at him over the noise. 'Who am I to care? I will be the first Dodwoman to absorb the Dragon's power into my mortal body. They shall be reborn and I shall be their leader. Here Be Dragons – and they are mine to command.'

And she stepped forward to grab him, to hurl him into the pits of hell. To appease the dragons and great beasts of Albion below, in their tombs.

'Down there, Robin. You are going down, down to meet the Dragons as they climb out after centuries of imprisonment!'

She was close to his face now. Oh yes, he was finally scared, finally ready to die at her triumph.

He leaned towards her, no doubt to beg one last time for mercy.

But she had no mercy. This was justice!

'Dodwoman, listen to me,' he was saying. 'There. Are. No. Dragons. They never existed – they are a fairy story to scare children.' And he laughed. 'And the Welsh.'

She laughed back. 'Of course. But the Dodpeople created the myth of the Dragon paths to access something through the very real ley lines they walked. The real ancient power. Vengeful spirits. The spirits of all the Dodpeople that came before. Betrayed, humiliated, executed for their beliefs over hundreds of years. And once they emerge from the chasm, they will share their generations of power – with me!'

Robin was trying to get out of her grasp. She could feel it through the ground, his feet teetering on the edge of a precipice, she could feel it pass through his body and into hers, the sensation of losing balance, of being ready to fall to the doom below.

'No!' he screamed at her. 'Don't you realise? Even if that were true, power such as that would be too strong for one person! That must be why the Dodpeople are always paired up. Alone with all that power you had… it sent you mad.

There, his footing was gone. Still linked to him, she could feel the sudden exhilaration as she fell.

'Mad!' she screamed back – why was his face still in front of hers? 'I am the one true power of Earth! I am—'

Then she realised her error. She had not felt Robin's loss of footing, she had not felt his exhalation of falling. She had felt her own, and he was holding her by her wrist.

Her thin, withered wrist, embittered and weakened by years of being kept alive by nothing but sheer anger and force of will – the will to remain alive until revenge was hers.

'Hold on, I'll pull you back up,' he was shouting.

'My people! The spirits of the past are coming! They will save me, fly me back up – we will yet have revenge on the blood of Loxley… I can hear them. They are COMING…'

She felt herself drop. And, in one last moment of clarity, she realised that her plan had failed. That Robin had lived, and it was her who was going to die.

A thought exemplified as the chasm gave a final shake and closed, crushing her useless aged body to dust in less than a heartbeat.

And her final thought was one of fury.

Where are my ancestors, she thought. Why have they betrayed me too?

And existence ended.

Further within Sherwood Forest, four hands were placed palm down, channelling their natural power, repairing and healing the forest, closing the chasms and rents that had been created.

And for one brief moment, the Woman in Green and Herne the Hunter worked in perfect tandem, to save Albion and the world.

CHAPTER SEVEN

R obin sat upright with a gasp.

There was air on his face and a slight damp within that air. He sniffed and smelled... freshness, cleanliness. Everything that wasn't the stench of a torn-apart earth.

He looked up into the black night. There were stars up there. Perhaps it was a good time to count them.

Perhaps not.

There was a voice coming through to him.

And he laughed. It was Little John. In his hand he carried Robin's sword.

'Robin! Robin, are you all right?'

'That sword came flying through the air,' wailed Tuck. 'It nearly took my head off.'

'It landed ten yards away,' grunted John. 'He was in more danger of cracking his head apart on a tree branch.'

Robin realised he was lying in Sam Tully's shallow grave. The Point of Power.

Of the destruction that the Scavenger had wrought upon the land, there was no sign.

It was as if it had never happened.

'Did we win?' asked Tuck. 'We have only just got poor Sam out of there.'

'We should give him a proper burial,' Robin muttered and noticed a look of satisfaction between Tuck and John. Clearly this had been a discussion.

'Did you witness the battle?' Robin asked his friends.

'Battle?'

'The ground, ripped asunder?'

Tuck and John looked at one another.

'Mayhaps a bump on the head?'

'Is the Scavenger gone?' asked John.

As Robin looked back at where he had lain, the ground slowly flowed back up, leaving no sign of the shallow grave or any indication where the Point of Power lay for future, unwary, wanderers.

'Perhaps it was another vision,' Robin suggested. 'But yes, the battle is won. We are safe.' He coughed. 'Head back to camp, I shall be ten paces behind you. I just need a moment alone.'

Tuck and John nodded their assent. 'We'll return tomorrow to bury poor Sam,' Tuck said, and he and John were gone, swallowed up by the darkness.

A safe darkness.

Robin sighed deeply. 'That. That was different.' He muttered aloud.

'We are so very proud of you, my son.'

Robin swung around. There, at the corner of his eye... he moved, but no, still there they were, in the corner. No matter how often he moved, they stayed just on the edge of sight, or on the edge of his mind.

'Mother? Father?'

'Your Mother and I love you and so I have been given permission to see you one last time.'

Lady Maire blew a kiss. 'Time to say a proper farewell.'

'But I... so much to say. To ask.'

'No Robin,' Lady Maire said. 'Tonight is about you moving forward, not backward. We are your past.'

'But,' Lord Ailric added with a smile and a twinkling eye, 'we shall always remain in your heart and memory.'

'Mother, Father, please...'

'We love you, son. It is time to go back to your friends. Quickly. And take care of yourself.'

All Robin could do was close his eyes, squeezing out tears, as he said one last time: 'I love you. So much... Thank you. For everything.'

And he knew they were gone.

Wiping his face with his sleeve, he gave the Point of Power one final glance. There was no sign anything had ever happened here.

And he followed the path taken by Tuck and John, into the woods and towards home.

***

A moment after Robin had gone, the air shimmered slightly and two figures stepped from previously unseen shadows and stood at the Point of Power.

'You are a good man, Herne,' said the Dodwoman, throwing her green hood away from her face one last time, feeling the air upon her skin. 'That was a kind gesture, letting him see his parents.'

'He deserved it. He is a true hero, which this land needs,' Herne growled.

The Dodwoman stepped directly onto the now unseeable Point of Power. 'You have taught him well and made him the man he needs to be. For all of us.'

Herne watched as she started to fade away, like dew on a morning breeze. 'What about you?' he asked.

She smiled. 'The Dragon lines still need guarding and mapping. My task is to appear to the next generation and guide them. Farewell Great Herne.'

And she was gone.

Herne bowed slightly at where she had stood. 'Farewell good Dodwoman. I will watch over Robin. And remember this day for despite all that has happened, this has merely been the calm before the final, tragic storm...'

You may also enjoy…

Richard Carpenter's
ROBIN OF SHERWOOD

THE RED LORD

Paul Kane

You may also enjoy…

Richard Carpenter's

ROBIN OF SHERWOOD

THE POWER OF THREE

Jennifer Ash